Reap What Has Been Sown
By Matt Kirkby

Copyright 2011 Matt Kirkby

Part One: Strike A Match
Chapter One

"I can see trouble brewing in your future."

"Put that stupid rock away."

"Do not mock the scrye stone. The scrye stone knows all."

"Shut up."

"It sees all."

"Shut up!"

"The scrye stone tells all."

"Shut up! Shut up! Shut up!"

Anton shook his head at the sounds of his two young apprentices bickering. "Janos! Keff! Both of you be quiet!" he snapped as he turned away from the chemical-stained desk. "By all the blessed Gods, how can I think with such incessant jabbering?" His eyes appeared to blaze with inner fire.

"Yes, Master." With a contrite bow, Janos hastily slipped the blue crystal back into his belt pouch.

Keff mimicked the bow. "Sorry, Master."

With a snort, Anton turned back to his desk and stared at the array of crystals and bottled potions strewn across its battered and age-worn surface. "'Tis a difficult enough task that I face, seeking out the keys to unlock the mysteries of the universe, without distractions from ungrateful and noisy apprentices."

"I told you that I could see trouble brewing in your future," Janos whispered.

"Shut up," Keff whispered back.

"We shall mix another batch of thunder dust," Anton said loudly. "Perhaps this time we will achieve some success."

"Yes, Master."

"Janos, see that the mixture is more finely ground than the last time."

"Yes, Master."

"Keff, set up the thunder tube."

"On the back balcony?"

"Of course I want it on the back balcony. Where else would I order it set, boy?" Anton shook his head. "*Apprentices*!" he made the word a curse. "By the Gods, 'tis no wonder that I am going gray!" He paused, but neither of his apprentices dared to comment. "How do you ever hope to learn anything?"

The only answer to his words was the tolling of the bell hung in the highest spire of the Temple.

* * *

"At least the neighbours do not complain."

"About what?" Anton demanded of his guest as the man peered around the cluttered workshop. "The so-called Perfumed Quarter is not known for the moral values or the class aspirations of its inhabitants." Far from it, the Gods' own truth be known. "The rent here is quite cheap," he admitted as he brushed lint from his blue sleeve. "The neighbors keep silent at odd noises and odder smells."

"And the Guards seldom patrol here." Anton's visitor wore the polished breastplate and leather skirt of a member of the City Guard.

Anton nodded. "Well, they used to be a rare sight. When I first started paying rent on this shop, there had not been a Guardsman sighted east of the Bridge of the Crimson Lady in nearly ten winters."

The other man chuckled bitterly. "That Bridge collapsed into the canal two nights ago."

"Did it really?" Anton blinked. "A pity that. The graffiti scrawled on its span was almost literate." That made it a rare thing indeed.

"Anyway...there are patrols from the Guards almost daily."

"'Tis the dark times we live in. Salidaralesom decays because no one will spare the funds to maintain it. Guardsmen patrol the streets to keep most of the citizens under control, rather than protecting the Empire from invaders. Ye Gods, the absurdity of it all astounds me even now! The Horde overwhelms our border provinces and raids deep into the heart of the Empire and only a token effort is made to slow them! The manpower kept here in this city is a crime. And for what? The nobles send out constant patrols to maintain the illusion that his Majesty still rules his own capitol."

"To hear such words from a captain in those very Guards does little to inspire my confidence, friend Mica."

"Should it?"

Anton refilled their mugs with the last of the sweet wine from the clay pitcher. He shrugged and scratched at his thigh.

Mica shifted position on the bench, trying to get more comfortable. Or to try and avoid splinters. "The only thing that gives me confidence is the thought of your invention."

"The thunder dust?"

"Aye. With that little trick, we can route the Horde and restore the Empire's borders to their former boundaries. Perhaps even expand them back to what they once were." He spoke wistfully at that. The boundaries had not grown in centuries...only contracted as various lands broke free from the fading Empire.

"Alas then for such dreams you have."

"Oh? Another tale of woe then?"

"Aye, for the latest round of experimentation has gone poorly. And so we have yet another delay facing us, friend Mica."

Mica shook his head. "Time is against us, Anton." He peered glumly into the depths of his clay mug as if the solution to all their problems could be found at the bottom of his wine. "The Horde is steadily advancing and the Guards are steadily retreating." He finished the wine in one gulp. "Always retreating."

"How grim are the tidings from the frontier?"

"The frontier is four hundred leagues closer than it was at winter's end. The Horde draws near to the fortress city of Tostoren."

"Ye Gods, they've reached the Gap of Tears already!" Anton nearly dropped his mug of wine. "At that rate, the Horde will be within bow shot of the city walls by next winter."

"Unless the Guard can field some advantage and hold them on the far side of the Gap." Mica tapped his breastplate. "I'm but a mere captain and I can plainly see the writing on the scroll...the city will fall."

"This is bad."

"Where are your apprentices?"

Anton blinked several times. "I sent them to the marker to buy some new supplies. Our mineral salts are running low. I cannot hope to create a working form of thunder dust without sulfur and the shipments from the mines have been disrupted of late."

"The Horde by land and pirates by sea."

"Aye. Pirates...."

"Your patron is having difficulty with the pirates, isn't he?"

"Aye, the damned Sea-Elves. Delmar has lost two cargoes in just this last moon. His finances are growing strained. Another lost cargo and he will be all but destitute." Anton shivered. "We will be patron less." The city would be hell itself for an unemployed scholar. *Slavery will become our fate...even before the Horde arrives.*

The door burst open. "Master, we're back!" Keff chirped happily as he walked in and dropped his sack onto the floor. "Hi, Mica. We found sulfur. And at a reasonable price for the quality."

"I trust that you checked inside the bags before paying any coins?" Anton demanded. "You did not pay for sulfur and purchase rock-salt."

"Of course not. Janos opened the sacks and checked."

"I did indeed, Master."

Anton grimaced. "Well at least one of you has a brain beneath those absurd hats." What had possessed the Empire's youth to wear such floppy hats and consider it the height of fashion was beyond his comprehension.

Mica grinned at the exchange. Janos and Keff were dissimilar in appearance and tastes, yet were fast friends. Janos was a slender blond youth who moved with surprising grace as if constantly dancing while red-haired Keff was of Hillman-stock and thus short, stocky, and usually walked as if daring something to stand in his path. *Yet they are fast friends. The fates are strange indeed.* Indeed, it was likely the two would set up shop somewhere following the eventual completion of their apprenticeship. *Assuming there is anything left of the Empire by then.*

"Have you heard word from the harbour?"

"No, Master. There is still no sign of Master Delmar's latest ship. The convoy is half a moon late. The storms have been fierce."

"One merchant claimed that Elf sorcerers were calling forth fierce storms to sink our ships."

"The Elves don't have that kind of power anymore." Anton chuckled grimly. "If they did, then they would never been overthrown by the merely Human ancestors of the Emperor."

Mica nodded his agreement. "It's been almost a thousand years since the conquest...if the Elves really had the power to cast such spells, surely they would have used them before now."

Janos frowned. "I never claimed to believe the rumour, I was merely repeating what I overheard in the market."

"Hearsay. Gossip! 'Tis not what I sent you out for."

"I know, Master."

Chapter Two

A cloud of acrid and bitter smoke rose from the metal pot on the table.

"'Tis another failure I think." Anton waved his hand through the smoke; vainly attempting to dispel the foul smelling fumes which billowed up around his head. "Open the shutters, boy!" he ordered.

"They are open!" Keff protested. "But there's no breeze."

"Damn." Anton abandoned his worktable and stumbled half-blind to the window. He blinked his eyes repeatedly to clear them, muttering curses under his breath.

A puff of breeze blew into the room.

He gazed through the open window for a moment and sighed softly. The Bay of Torenth—just glimpsed between two rather decrepit apartment blocks—looked blue and inviting. "Check the thunder tube for damage." Keff hurried off to obey.

"We *are* getting close."

Anton turned. "What makes you so confident, Apprentice?"

Janos grinned. "This batch smells better than the last one did."

Out on the balcony, Keff laughed loudly.

"I seek power, not sweet perfume!" Anton snapped. *Apprentices! Why do I torment myself with such donkey-brained fools?*

"We meddle with forces only barely understood, Master. Any success should come slowly."

Anton was momentarily speechless as he considered that statement. "An astute observation. For once."

Janos grinned. *Praise with one hand and a rebuke with the other. Typical for my esteemed and all-knowing Master.* "Thank you."

"Now if we could just figure out the rest of this mess."

"What's that noise?" Anton asked as a dull roar came through the windows on the other side of the house.

"Ye Gods, another riot." Keff turned from the desk.

"They're becoming a daily occurrence." The streets of Salidaralesom were becoming unsafe to travel by day or night.

"I'll check on things." Keff quickly ran across the worn floorboards to the front window. "I can see torches!" he called out.

"They'll burn down the neighborhood." Anton looked around, noting his mineral salts and oil drums and mounds of other equipment and supplies. "Gods preserve us! This place will go up like an oil-soaked rag."

"Do not fear, Master," Janos kept his voice calm, masking his own fear. "I have placed wards around this house." He spoke with confidence, though he was not completely certain that he had pronounced all of the mystical words correctly. *I need a living teacher,* he thought bitterly, *not just reading scraps picked out from old scrolls.*

"Janos, your wards will not save us." Anton shook his head at his apprentice's aspirations towards the magical arts. "The old Gods have forsaken us just as the Emperor's priests keep saying."

"Never." Janos shook his head. "The old Gods are testing us." They had to be. "Or maybe they're sleeping again. Progenatorum slept through the birth of the universe after all."

"Your youthful confidence will not carry you through every adversity."

"Better that than despair!"

"Watch your tongue."

"Would you have me cower under the bed like some old maid?"

"The mob is moving towards the Tenth Vintner's Street," Keff reported happily as he stepped away from the window. He didn't seem to have been paying attention to the brewing argument. "We're safe."

Anton rolled his eyes towards the heavens. "Mobs, fire, and wine. What a wonderful combination."

* * *

"Elf!" The shout echoed through the marketplace, followed by the cry of "Thief". They cut through the near-constant shouts of fishmongers and tinkers and tailors.

The blond man in a grimy brown cloak tried to run, but failed to reach the first bridge before two armour-clad Guardsmen seized his arms. A crowd began to gather around him, almost immediately.

Three more Guardsmen approached in their polished breastplates, black leather skirts and blue cloaks, as did the woman who had given the initial shout.

"You are certain, Mistress?" Mica asked her in a calm voice. He watched one of his fellows place chains on the accused man's wrists.

"I am. He is the one who accosted me." She smoothed her green dress with a haughty air. "I will swear such before the Emperor himself. The dirty Elf should be hung."

"His fate will be decided by the Imperial Magistrates."

"Not every man with blond hair is an Elf."

Mica turned to look at the accused, surprised that he had spoken up. "Maybe not, sir."

The man rattled his chains. "I protest this treatment."

"Maybe every man is not an Elf," Mica said, "but you *are* a thief."

"I stole nothing!" the accused shouted. "I am innocent." The rest of the marketplace seemed to ignoring his protests. "I am a loyal citizen. I pay my taxes. I pay your salary, Guardsman!"

Mica shook his head as the man was dragged away by two of the Guards, followed by the woman who still vowing in a loud shrill voice that he was guilty. "The magistrate will deal with him," he said to himself as the peddlers and fishmongers began shouting again.

"I trust he will actually receive justice."

With a sudden smile on his face, Mica turned to the speaker. "Janos, I had not thought to see you here." Mica hurriedly clasped his friend on his shoulder. "What brings you abroad on such a day?"

"The need for supplies." Janos gave the marketplace a sharp look. "Though I find the prices to be growing faster than the weeds in what should be my herb garden."

"The prices grow as the Empire shrinks."

Janos ran a hand nervously through his rather scraggly beard.

Mica noticed the gesture and laughed. "Do you hope that such facial fur makes you appear more scholarly?"

"No, Mica, I rather hope that it masks my heritage." He kept his voice low to avoid being overheard by passersby. "The Empire grows ever less friendly to my kin." No one seemed inclined to linger and listen to their conversation but he still exercised caution.

The manner in which Mica rested his hand on the sword belted to his waist most likely encouraged passersby to keep moving. "The Court is worried," he agreed in a low voice.

"The whole city is worried." Janos darted several nervous looks around the marketplace. "Rumours are flying into the city about another series of raids against the border forts."

"They are not just rumours."

The grim certainty in his friend's tone gave Janos a start. "Then the rumour was true?"

Mica nodded, his smile turned to a grim frown. "Tostoren has fallen to the Keli'cairn Horde."

Chapter Three

"This mixture will work."

The sound of voices arguing echoed from within the House.

Anton gestured. "Fetch me a candle."

"You don't plan to test it here?" Janos protested. *Surely I heard him wrong?* "Not in the heart of the city! Not in our patron's House." This was why they kept their labouratorium in the poor district...where the neighbors were much less likely to complain at the odd sounds and smells that emanated from their property at times. *Of course, the neighbors do a lot of their own emanating.*

"I shall test the thunder dust wherever I please." Anton drew his blue and green robes around himself. "This time the mixture will work."

"As you wish, Master." Janos shook his head. Master Delmar would not be pleased at having his afternoon rest disturbed by an explosion in his scholar's workshop. *Of course, whomever he is arguing with will keep him from slumbering.* He couldn't make out any of the words, but he could hear the raised voices. *Quite the heated discussion going on in there.* Janos nervously rubbed a hand through his beard.

"Our patron wishes to see profits from this venture." Anton was in one of his moods. "He will not waste more coin on idle speculation and foolishness. He was most insistent on that point."

Janos sighed. *I knew that morning interview was not going to be a good one. Delmar is growing poor and he's growing desperate to recoup his fading fortunes.* Status was everything these days and Delmar's formerly important House was quickly losing its luster.

"When the thunder dust proves itself successful, we will supply the Imperial Army with the means to throw back the Horde and regain all of its lost territories. Master Delmar will rise in importance and he will reward his loyal servants appropriately." Anton picked up one of his vials. "Why, Delmar might even be appointed a minister or chamberlain. Think of how he would reward us then!"

"Indeed." Janos didn't know what else to say.

The door to the main house creaked opened and a terrified looking housekeeper scurried out into the courtyard.

"You are not permitted in here!" Anton thundered at her. "Get out of my workshop."

The housekeeper was crying and took no notice of his imperious orders or his rude gesturing. Her white hair had broken free from its usual severe bun and was flying loosely.

"What is going on?" Janos asked her in a gentle voice.

"'Tis awful," she wailed.

"Gods, spare me from women and plague!" Anton grumbled, turning back to his powders and notes.

"What has happened?" Janos asked in a soft voice as he led the old woman away from the corner where their workshop was located.

She looked at him and blinked her watery eyes. "The Guardsmen, sir, they've come for us."

"What Guardsmen?"

"The Imperial Guardsmen. Master Delmar has defaulted."

Janos paled. "*Defaulted*?" he repeated.

"Aye."

Janos felt the cold chill from the hearts of the deepest winter settle into his chest. "Surely the Merchant's Guild—"

"Has already sent the Guardsmen to arrest Delmar and his family." Keff hurried into view. He looked back over his shoulder. "Who do you think Delmar is arguing with." The voices inside the house had fallen silent. "I was in the kitchen, getting myself a snack, and listening in."

"We'll be patron less!" Janos gasped out the first thought to enter his head. "Cast out onto the street!" *I can't make a decent living begging for crumbs and coins!*

"Nay, we'll be seized to cover the debt!"

"Aye," the housekeeper wailed, "we'll be sold at auction. Raped in our beds."

"Bloody unlikely for you," Keff muttered under his breath.

"Good mistress, calm yourself." Janos patted her arm. "The Merchants will be understanding."

"No they won't. The Guardsmen are here to ensure the household is seized according to the Law. We're to be sold in auction to pay the debts."

Anton stormed up to his two apprentices and the shaking housekeeper. "What are you two going on about?" he demanded. "Can I not have peace in my own workshop?"

"Delmar's workshop," Keff pointed out. "It is his House after all."

"Quiet you."

"The Guards have come to arrest Delmar in default for his loans—"

"Nonsense. Master Delmar's finances are quite stable. For now. He told me so himself this morning." Anton snorted loudly. "I cannot work with all this mindless chatter distracting me. How the two of you expect to learn anything of note from me while you make all that noise is quite beyond me. And you," Anton rounded on the still-sobbing housekeeper, "this courtyard and the contents of my workshop are sacrosanct! Get out!"

The housekeeper fled.

"Now then—"

"But what about the Guardsmen, Master?"

"Now then," Anton repeated, "I have a new mixture of thunder dust to test. The Guardsmen can wait if they wish to see me."

The door to the house opened and four Imperial Guardsmen in full uniform stepped into the courtyard, blinking in the warm sunlight. "Master Anton Millerson?"

"I am he." Within the confines of his workshop, Anton stood as regal as the emperor himself in his dusty robes. He stared down his nose at the four interlopers.

"We are here to oversee the dispersal of the household contents and staff in lieu of debts incurred by Master Delmar."

Anton drew himself to his full height. "I am a freeman."

The Guardsman nodded politely. "And you have papers stating such?" He rested his hand on his sheathed sword.

"Of course. Not on me at the moment; they must be in my workshop near the harbour." Anton gestured back towards the house. "The household secretary would have a copy in his records."

"The secretary has proven unwilling to reveal himself."

"That is hardly my concern," Anton replied coldly.

Janos felt a tug at his tunic.

"Let's run," Keff whispered.

"We can't." The Guards were watching.

"I am no mere slave to be ordered around," Anton was telling the Guardsman in a loud and arrogant tone. "And the contents of my workshop are my own."

"The records stating such will have to be seen."

"All that you see here is mine. Don't touch that!" Anton reached for the pottery jug one of the Guardsmen had picked up to examine. "Foolish oaf! There be dangerous elements within my workshop."

"'Tis only a black powder." The Guardsman tossed the jug back onto the table.

"No, you fool!" Anton shrieked. The jug shattered and black gritty powder scattered across the table in little puffs of dust. One cloud gusted into a guttering candle.

A tremendous roar filled the workshop.

The tolling of the Temple bell was almost as loud as the ringing in his ears. Janos coughed on the thick smoke that filled the air. "By all the gods," he cursed as he stood up. "Master?" he called out. "Keff?" The crack of falling masonry warned him that the building was no longer stable.

"Did we just get smote by the War God's own Hammer?" Keff asked as he stood up. He tried to brush dust from his tunic but it was a futile effort. "Wow!" he gasped.

Most of the workshop was in ruins. The long workshop table and its contents was gone, with only a few splintered shards of wood left to mark where it had once stood.

Of Master Anton, there was no sign.

"Ye Gods," Janos muttered. "The thunder dust worked far more powerfully than we though."

"The Guardsmen are dead." Crouching beside one of the only two Guardsmen still visible, Keff shook his head. "This is not good." He stood up and hurriedly stepped away from the bleeding corpse. "We're gonna get blamed for this."

"But who is going—"

"We've got to get out of here." Keff waved at a wisp of lingering smoke. "The priests will call it black magic of the darkest arts. We're gonna be hung."

"If we're lucky." Janos felt a chill at the thought. "The priests will probably execute us with something really nasty." He shivered. "The newest batch is the most strict."

"That's what you get when you listen to this One God silliness," Keff told him. "No one god can oversee everything in creation. Everyone knows you need lots of gods. Especially with the Horde overrunning the border provinces...the Emperor and his priests should be praying to each and every single god and goddess who will listen."

"Maybe." Janos pulled open the drawer of a fallen-over cabinet. It was sticking and he tugged harder at the handle. "Gather up what you can." He began stuffing scrolls into a small bag. "We'll have to hide out in the labourtorium." He tried to gather up the most valuable scrolls. *Who can tell what is most valuable?* he wondered. *I can't save everything.* "What will Delmar do?" Assuming he could fend off the debt collectors with promises or partial payments or something. "Gods, he'll be blamed for this mess too! Charges of black sorcery!"

"That is his concern. We need to hide before more Guardsmen show up."

"We can't use the front door."

"The housekeeper." Keff looked around but there was no sign of her. "Where did she get too?"

"Probably slipped out the back."

"Of course. The back gate," Keff slapped his forehead. "I should have guessed. I caught her there once with one of the butcher's delivery boys." He shuddered at the memory. "Gods, she was old enough to be his grandmother."

"Yep." Janos looked around the rubble. *So much to save,* he thought grimly, *and us with no time at all.*

The back gate opened up into an alley that would not have been out-of-place in the city's lower neighborhoods. Almost immediately Janos felt his boot sink into something squishy and wished that he could stop breathing as the stench rose around him.

"We have to hurry."

"I know. I know." Edging around the side of the wall, he stared into the main street. "It's bad."

The far end of the street had been blocked by a restless crowd and it was very quickly growing ugly. A handful of Imperial Guardsmen were present, forming an unstable wall against the debt collectors and ordinary citizens. One Guardsman was pounding, grim-faced, on the door of the house. Shouts about witchcraft were being raised by the crowd.

The stench of sulfur was hanging in the air.

Janos gave a jump as a hand latched onto his arm.

"What is going on?"

"Mica!" Janos felt a surge of relief as he focused on the man holding his arm. "Anton blew himself up!"

"And took out four Guardsmen," Keff added.

"What? How?"

"An accident with the thunder dust." Janos shivered. "It was awful."

"And that was before the debt collectors came."

"I see." Mica surveyed the scene down the street. "You two get over to my house now. We'll talk in depth tonight." Waving his sword in the air, Mica hurriedly strode towards the crowd. "Order!" he shouted in his best parade ground voice. "Order! In the name of his Majesty, I will have order." Shouts and curses answered his cries.

Keff hurried down the street. Janos followed, though more slowly. He scarcely noticed five Temple Guardsmen—immaculate in pristine white robes and recently polished mail—hurry past. Delmar had been his patron for many years...since he had first convinced Anton to take him on as an apprentice in the Natural Sciences. He stopped to take one last look at the house.

Smoke was rising from behind the wall.

Chapter Four

"The fire was fairly small," Mica told them that night, "but it burned the living quarters almost to ash. I organized a fire brigade and we saved most of the house."

"And what of our patron?"

"Delmar the Elder was dead...though from a knife in the heart."

"Ye Gods."

"It looks to have been suicide, Janos. It was his ceremonial jeweled dagger and his own hand still clenched at the hilt. Mistress Delmar had taken poison."

"Ye Gods," Keff repeated.

"And their children?" Janos asked softly.

Mica took a long moment before answering.

"Poison again," Janos answered his own question with a wince. *Why*? "How could this have happened?"

"Ill-luck with his trading ventures."

"Those damned pirates!" Keff swore. "Where is the Fleet when you need it? What do we pay taxes for?"

"Since when do you pay taxes?" Janos asked.

"Well...."

"The Fleet patrols where it can but the Sea of Storms is vast. Pirates strike almost at will." Mica frowned at them both. "And taxes help fund the Imperial Guard as well as the Navy." He lifted his clay mug. "So enjoy the wine I bought with my pay from the taxes you never paid." He and Keff laughed and toasted each other.

Janos shook his head, ignoring their merriment. "Where do the pirates come from? That's what I want to know."

"Pirates...Sea-Elves. Both one and the same pretty much."

"Not so, Keff. The Sea-Elves hold to a code of honor. But it is *Elf* honor. They see themselves as privateers more than pirates. Or so I have been told."

Janos gave Mica an appraising glance. "Since when do you know so much about the doings and nature of the Sea-Elves?"

Mica shrugged. "The Lord-Admiral gave a small talk at a recent luncheon. I listened...his speech was more entertaining than the songs of the hired minstrels. A pity the food was little better than the local taverns could have provided."

"Ah, I see."

"So the question remains." Keff set down his mug. "If the Empire controls the Fleet and the Fleet patrols the Sea so well, then where do the pirates hide?"

"The Sea of Storms is a big place. Lots of islands I would imagine."

"The harbour of Meerlasynth shelters the bulk of the Emperor's Fleet." Mica waved his hand off to the west. "I have heard that it is supposedly the greatest harbour in the world. A sheltered cove, guarded against attack from both land and sea."

"I would like to travel there some day. Assuming the Horde doesn't burn it."

"The Horde doesn't bother with boats. Never had much need for them on the edge of the Waterless Wastelands after all. What they will do with Meerlasynth is anyone's guess right now." Mica was staring off into distant space, his eyes unfocused.

"We need to find a new patron." Janos brought the discussion back to the matter at hand. *Talking of the fleet will do us little good.*

"And quickly."

"I have spoken with the clerk of records."

"Already?"

"Before the afternoon ended. After the fire was subdued, the debt collectors became insistent on recovering their payments from the house and whatever household slaves they could seize. I had the Guards hold them back, but I could only delay the looting."

"I see." Janos wondered how many of his friends in the Delmar household had been enslaved by other masters. *Will I ever see them again*? he wondered. *Or worse, will I be joining them in slavery?* He devoutly hoped not.

"The Minister of Justice was too busy to deal with our petitions, of course, but one of the lesser Ministers saw us. I was able to see the list of debts." Mica paused a moment, staring down into his wine. "The chief debt-keeper is Colm Barrelweight."

"By the Gods, not the Vulture!" Keff moaned and collapsed into his chair. "No wonder Delmar killed himself."

Janos sipped at his wine to buy himself time for thought. "The man our patron died to escape is our best hope of a new patron?"

"He is the richest of the debt collectors. His staff has been plundering most of the items recovered from the house. Sadly, he has the bulk of your equipment and supplies, even though he lacks the skills to use them. He will need you."

"The Gods have a cruel sense of humour."

* * *

"At least the Vulture's house is on the nice side of the canal."

Janos glanced over his shoulder and grimaced. "This is the tenth canal we've crossed today!"

"The Topaz Bridge is much nicer than the Garnet Bridge or even the Sapphire Bridge," Keff continued. "And immeasurably better than the Perfumed Quarter."

"The Perfumed Quarter should be renamed the Sewage Sink."

Mica snorted.

Janos eyed the canal, ignoring the passersby. The water looked murky, though still cleaner than the canal closest to their labouratorium. *Is that a rat*? He stopped for a moment to stretch the kinks from his back and straighten out his tunic. He and Keff had both taken care to dress in their finest garments...but neither man owned much fashionable wear. *At least our tunics are clean.*

Mica had chosen to wear his Guardsman's uniform. The breastplate was newly polished—how the housekeeper had complained about the efforts required of her the previous evening after supper—and the leather skirt hung to his knees.

"It's got a good view of the Citadel."

Janos looked. The Emperor's Citadel rose above the rest of the city. Built atop a hill around which the capitol sprawled, the Citadel was a city unto itself. Walled in gray stone, it was the city's last line of defence, the center of law and order for the Empire.

"Untouchable."

"Doomed if the Horde comes." Mica spat into the canal. "If the city's walls fall, I doubt those will stand any longer."

"The Emperor will not allow Salidaralesom to fall. His One God will protect him."

"One God or many," Mica said, "I've yet to see divine intervention defeat an army."

A white-robed priest strode past them.

* * *

"Mica Swordson, Captain of his august Majesty's Imperial Guard to see Colm Barrelweight."

The door warden peered out at him. "A moment, good Captain." The wizened ancient within let the spy-hole close with a soft thump.

"Now what?" Keff asked as the wait lengthened.

"We continue to wait patiently," Mica told them.

"Or else we could demonstrate the effectiveness of the thunder dust by blowing a hole in this wall." Janos chuckled at the thought. The house, like most of those owned by wealthy merchants, was hidden behind a tall gray stone wall. It seemed to sit and wait with ominous foreboding.

"That might not be the best means of gaining an audience," Mica pointed out. "Fast, but not effective."

Keff shrugged. "It was just a thought." He watched people walking along the street. "They look like a good class."

"We are so out of place here." Janos took a deep breath. "I hate interviews with new patrons."

The bronze-sheathed doors slowly creaked open. "The Master will see you." The warden offered them a shallow bow.

Janos eyed the man as he passed. *He must be about eighty.*

"This way, good masters."

The interior of the house was gray and dusty. It was decorated, though the statues, pottery, and the occasional tapestry on the wall seldom shared the same style.

The looting of how many debtors? Janos wondered grimly.

"This place is only gray...did the Vulture banish all colour?"

"Quiet!" Mica hissed at Keff.

The corridor opened into a small courtyard with a pond in its center to catch the rain. Beyond the small pond, a locked door waited.

The porter tapped at the door.

"Enter!" a harsh voice commanded.

Janos followed Mica into what was obviously the office for Colm.

The walls were lined with shelves of scrolls and tablets. An abacus waited on a small table, flanked by two sets of scales. A few bags of coins and jewels were strewn about, adding to the impression of a place of wealth.

The bulk of his ready money must be elsewhere, Janos guessed. *Surely he would not leave* all *of his wealth laying about.* Though given the Vulture's reputation, Janos had expected to find the man resting upon a mound of coins like some fearsome dragon of myth.

Colm was old, with his obese body mostly hidden by a fur-trimmed cloak, drawn up around himself. His bald head gleamed in the candlelight.

Mica offered him a polite bow. "Good day, Master Money Lender."

"Good day to you, Captain. What brings you to my abode on this fine day? Do you seek to borrow funds? I have had traffic with the Imperial Court and they know me to be an honest man."

"I am not here on business for myself, Master Colm, but rather I come to you on business of the Court." Which was partially truth. "I am told that you were owed money by the Merchant, Delmar."

"Yes, and I did not recover the full amount of the debt owed to me due to his death." Colm leaned forward, his robe straining against his voluminous belly. "What little I took from the house will fetch a mere pittance in the market places of the city."

"I have consulted with the record clerks." Mica tapped the rolled up scroll he had stuck into his belt. "I have the listing of the total debts and how much has been recovered thus far."

Colm eyed the scroll with avid hunger.

"I present to you Janos Feldspar, and his apprentice Keff Redstone."

Janos bowed carefully. He looked older than Keff, though not by much. *I hope he believes me to be the master. No one would believe Keff is the master of us both.* He hoped that Mica's housekeeper had laundered his robes clean enough to pass Colm's scrutiny.

Colm's eyes narrowed as he studied the two young men. "And why do you bring them to me, Guardsman Captain?"

"You are wealthy, and looking to become wealthier. These two are valuable craftsmen and learned scholars. It seems a fair trade to place them within your care."

Colm's eyes narrowed further. "Can you speak on your own behalf?"

"Of course, my lord." Janos kept his tone differential. *I shall grovel if I must.* "In the simplest terms, my assistant and myself require a patron."

Colm blinked his watery eyes. "You want money."

"A pittance, Good Master." *He does look a like a vulture.* "A few crowns to purchase supplies for our studies. A few coins to pay the rent on our humble labouratorium near the harbour."

"And you would promise me what prizes in return for this *pittance*?"

"Our skills." Janos drew himself straighter. "We have knowledge of spells and potential devices that could save the Empire from the Horde!"

Colm said nothing. His narrowed eyes closed even more.

Janos looked at Keff for a quick reassurance.

"That would be well worth the gamble of a few crowns." As the three wondered who had made that observation, a young woman with fiery red hair brushed past Mica to move to Colm's side. She studied the two scholars and their escort with a bold stare from her blue eyes. A slight tilt to her eyes betrayed at least a hint of Elf-Blood in her heritage.

"Perhaps, Sapphire." Colm seemed unconvinced. His eyes lacked any of the Elf-Blood tilt.

"There are scholars beyond count these days. They multiply in our midst like so many locusts. Why should I fund the idle musings of two more?"

"The furtherance of education and the spreading of knowledge are things to be prized, dear brother. Knowledge is a finer treasure than any jeweled bauble within your cellars."

Brother? Janos traded surprised glances with Keff. *I didn't know he had a sister.*

"So you claim," Colm continued.

"A small expense could reap much wealth in return should their skills prove as great as they claim."

"And if not, then I am wasting money for no gain. Why should I waste seed without reaping a harvest?"

Mica offered a short bow to him. "If you are not interested, Master Barrelweight, then I apologize for wasting your time. I will take these two along to another on my list. Perhaps one of the other debt collectors will gamble the coins on reaping the profits of their work."

Colm blinked.

"Surely we would not wish that." The woman smiled. "After all, 'tis only a pittance they ask."

"Perhaps I will consider taking them into my household," Colm said at last. "In interest of securing the monies owed to me by their former patron," he added hastily. "I will expect a return on my investment."

"I trust that your reward will be all that your deserve," Mica told him with a bow.

Chapter Five

"Most of the workshop is here." Keff set a model onto a shelf, and then tried to pull a different one from the pile of assorted wooden scraps.

Janos dug through a bundle of scrolls. "It looks that way." Did Colm get everything? "Where is that cursed scroll on the lenses? Surely we didn't leave it behind?"

"I saw it in that pile." Keff gestured to a stack of scrolls. One of many such stacks they had scrounged. "How can you worry about the lenses?"

"Colm hired us to complete our far-seers. I need to check on the curvature of the glass in the lenses."

"Lenses be damned!" Keff snapped. "Do you think we will have the money to finish our true work?"

"Perhaps."

"If not, then how do we work on the thunder dust?"

"I'm not sure I want to," Janos replied softly.

"Not sure?" Surprised, Keff dropped the wooden model out of his hands. "But the thunder dust is to be the fulfillment of our life's work! It'll save the Empire."

"It killed Anton!" Janos took care to lower his voice. Although their new workshop was located in a back corner of the house property, he still took care in case of spies. "You saw Delmar's workshop." He shuddered at the memory of that explosion.

"That was an accident."

"And what an accident!"

"We'll be more careful."

"Ye Gods, Keff." Janos dropped the scrolls onto the floor. "I wish that I could share your confidence."

"We're going to be famous."

"We're going to be cursed! We are trifling with dangerous forces, Keff, very dangerous forces. Anton was careless and look at what happened to him! The Priests are still preaching against the use of the Dark Arts."

"It was chemistry, not sorcery."

"It looks like dark magic! The War God's fist smote the workshop and destroyed half of Delmar's house."

"We survived. We'll learn from our mistakes. We are going to be okay, Janos. The thunder dust will work. It has too."

Janos shook his head. "Don't you ever get depressed?"

"Nope."

* * *

"This is but one of our experiments in progress, good Master."

"Get on with it." Colm squinted in the morning sun. He did seem happy with the fine weather. Sweat beaded his brow and dripped from his nose.

Janos felt like sighing. He had waited through three long days of rain for good weather so that he could display his far-seer. *Will nothing make the Old Vulture happy?* he wondered in annoyance.

Sapphire smiled encouragement to him.

"I would like to point out the care required to shape the glass just so." Janos held one of the delicate lenses between the thumb and first finger of his right hand. "They are smoothed only by much polishing." Many, many man-hours of careful polishing. *Ye Gods, I care never to polish so much as a spoon again!* "They are fitted thusly, within this leather tube." He rolled the strip of leather into a tube with a lens at either end. "And when you hold it to your eye, it brings things close enough to touch."

Colm took the tube and held it up to his watery eye. "Ye Gods," he swore aloud. "The Citadel is so close." He took the tube from his eye and peered up at the Emperor's home once again distant. "What a fine trick!"

"'Tis only a small toy," Janos continued. "Imagine how far one could gaze with a larger tube?" *And larger lenses...which would require far more polishing.*

Colm was staring through the tube at the Temple of the One God. "I can see its potential. Yes, I can see the Bell of Invocation!"

And the wealth it could bring, Janos finished the thought for himself. "Aye, good Master. Mounted upon a ship, the captain could see pirates long ere they could attack. A general with a far-seer tube could place his troops to best fight an enemy before said enemy could see them."

"Yes," Colm mused, "I do see the potentials to come from this humble toy of yours."

* * *

Dinner that night was more lively than most.

Colm and his sister were entertaining.

"One of the Lord-Captains of the Guardsmen." The scullery maid pointed to the man seated to Colm's right. "Two of his aides and clerks. A captain from one of Colm's more successful galleons and other sundry ship-mates."

Janos nodded. "An august company for our master."

"They have come to see your little toy."

"The far-seer tube." Keff snickered and reached for more of the hard yellow cheese. "The simplest of our toys."

"The profits to come will make our master happy." Janos emptied his mug and grimaced at the dryness of the wine.

"And thus will make our lives a bit easier. The Gods be praised." The clerk refilled Janos's mug. "For that, we thank you."

"The Old Vulture isn't so bad."

"Yes he is. But keep him happy and he'll let you alone." The gray-haired cook glanced up at the main table where Colm was talking to his guests and smiled shyly. "We all cover for each other...it makes the household run more smoothly."

"Good thinking." Keff nodded.

"And this is the man who invented the far-seer tubes." Colm gestured to the servants' table. "Janos, come here!"

Reluctantly leaving his half-eaten dinner, Janos hurried to the table and bowed appropriately. "Master. My Lords. Mistress." He bowed again.

"We have been testing your far-seer from the west balcony," the Lord-Captain said in a gruff tone. "I am most impressed. The scouts of our corps of Guards will be doubly efficient now in their missions. A fine job." He pulled a coin from his pouch and tossed it to Janos.

"Thank you, my Lord Captain." With a bow, Janos stuffed the coin into his belt-pouch.

"How long would it take you to produce more of these tubes?"

"A few weeks. The most time-consuming part is the polishing."

"And the making of the glass for the lenses?"

"Any glassmaker in the city could make them," Janos informed them. "And polish them. My assistant and myself can show anyone the basics of making the tubes."

"I will not have every glassmaker in the city selling the secrets of the far-seer tubes to anyone who asks," Colm growled. "The secret stays within this House."

"Indeed," the Lord Captain nodded. "His Imperial Majesty would not care to see these tubes appearing in the hands of our enemies. Still, he would also prefer to see more tubes appear quickly so that they might be issued to our scouts. Two craftsman cannot work fast enough to supply far-seers in such numbers."

"Perhaps we could replace some of our departed household servants with skilled glassmakers who have fled here as refugees?"

Colm looked at his sister in surprise.

She returned his gaze with a calm smile. "They would come cheaply enough, I trust, and grateful for a roof over their heads and food in their bellies."

"No, Sapphire, I will not spend the coins on more idle hands."

"As you wish." She paused a moment. "Perhaps his Majesty's Guards can supply more able hands to work upon these tubes."

The Lord-Captain nodded. "There are many conscripts who could stand to perform honest work in lieu of stumbling about the battlefield."

"We shall discuss the supply of workers later," Colm said. "As well as at what price the tubes will be sold. And who will pay for the supplies and costs of feeding these *conscripts* as they labour."

"As they will be working to supply the Guards, the conscripts will be cared for by the Guards."

"And the cost of supplies?"

"The tubes are equipping the Imperial Guardsmen. The Empire will supply your needs...for a fair price."

A greedy light appeared within Colm's eyes. "Perhaps I would prefer to supply my own needs...and charge a fair price for the completed tubes."

The Captain leaned forward. "I should like to hear your *fair* price."

"Good Master?" Janos interrupted. "I would speak with you about another of my inventions."

"Later, Janos."

"But this invention could save the Empire."

"Later I said." There was a dangerous gleam in Colm's eye, replacing the earlier greed.

"This cannot wait." Janos threw a small packet of parchment into one of the torches. A flash of blue fire erupted, with a thick cloud of smoke.

The men seated at the table leaped to their feet with many curses and cries. The servants cowered at their table. Colm's sister alone remained seated, calmly watching.

"You keep a wizard?" the Lord-Captain demanded as he grabbed for his sword. His aides had already drawn their daggers and held them ready for use.

"Of course not." Colm was glaring at Janos. "'Tis only my fool scholar playing with some foul potion or other."

"My—" Janos fell silent as the full weight of his master's glare settled onto him.

"Get out of my sight!" Colm snarled. "Now!" he thundered.

Janos fled.

Chapter Six

"It is not fair!" Janos cursed as he threw a pottery jar against the wall with a crash. "Not fair at all!"

"Calm yourself," Keff soothed as he stepped into the room and closed the door behind him. "You'll wake the entire house with that racket." He held up his candle. The place was a big a mess as the sound had led him to suspect. Toppled shelves, scattered scrolls and parchments. Broken pottery.

"How can you be so calm?" Janos demanded. "The Vulture refused to see what I tried to show him. He only saw the far-seer as a toy. After my ill-fated demonstration at dinner, he'll never fund our work on the thunder dust."

"Maybe we can find the funds elsewhere?"

"We aren't allowed to leave the house grounds." Janos snorted. "I am forbidden to leave my quarters."

Keff lit a second candle as Janos turned to pace back-and-forth across the chamber. "We'll find a way. More of Anton's learned tricks mayhap?" he suggested. "Pad our requests for supplies, steal whatever else we need from the household stores."

"Just like old times."

"Yep. Just like old—by the Gods!" Keff cursed. "What happened to your face?"

Janos froze in mid-step. "I had forgotten you did not see me earlier."

"Who did this too you?" Keff eyed the bruises on his friend's face then the answer came to him. "Our *Master*?"

"An outward sign of his displeasure."

"That—"

"I have taken some herbs. I'll be fine."

Keff shook his head. "How could he do this to you?"

"It doesn't matter."

"But..."

"I said it doesn't matter." Janos blew out the candle. "Leave me alone."

Keff shook his head.

* * *

"I have heard it said that the lady of the house has her own source of funds."

Janos looked up from the scroll he was reading. "She does?"

"Aye, or so the second scullion told me."

"I thought you were spending more time than usual in the kitchens."

Keff shrugged and brushed his red hair out of his face. "Colm keeps a well-stocked larder."

"Be cautious that he doesn't catch you within his larder else you might end up hanging amongst the hams and chickens."

"I am careful. Serai would warn me if the old Vulture was on the prowl." Keff carefully mixed two chemicals together and watched them do absolutely nothing. "Wrong mix," he muttered.

"I suggest that you stay away from the scullions."

"I like Serai. She's a very nice girl. Plump in all the right places. And she loves to canoodle."

Janos shook his head. "You and her are spending time cuddling up in Colm's chair and playing 'master of the house'?"

"Sometimes."

"The Gods spare me details of your latest conquest. I am thankful that the walls of our bedchambers are thick." Janos made a notation on the tablet in front of him. "Leaving the kitchen larder and the scullion behind, what else did you learn of the Lady's financial resources?"

"She is known to fund certain projects on her own initiative."

"Where does she get the money?"

"No one knows."

"I doubt she's a woman of the streets." Janos could not picture the gentle Sapphire working the street trade. "Family wealth do you think?'

"Possibly." Keff picked up a different vial and poured into the first batch. "She is of Elf-Blood I think. Many of them had wealth before the Empire conquered them."

"Or maybe she simply gambles on the returns of her projects? But where did the first coins come from with which she could fund her pursuits? I say, do you think that she—ye Gods!"

Keff stared glumly at the bubbling goop dissolving a hole in the table top.

"What are you doing?"

"I don't think these chemicals are the right ones. This was not the effect I was trying for."

"Be careful! Mess up with the thunder dust and you're likely to kill us all."

"Stop worrying so much. I have everything under control."

* * *

Janos was standing next to the garden fountain, listening to the water splashing softly into the basin, when the lady of the household slowly approached. *At least my bruises have faded*, he thought. *Merely leaving me with the memories of a week of pain.*

Sapphire's pace slowed as she caught sight of her servant standing ahead of her. "Why do you disturb my nightly walk?" she asked. The ruby ring on her finger was sparkling softly.

"I must speak with you...and I wished to do so in private."

"Walk with me then." She paced slowly through the garden, stopping once to brush her hands through a patch of lavender to enjoy the scent as it wafted into the air.

"I have heard rumours, my Lady," Janos began. "We are told that you have access to certain funds."

Night birds chirped softly.

"So my brother was correct…you do wish money."

Janos nodded. "A pittance, my Lady. Enough to pay the rent on our small workshop down by the harbour. Enough to buy certain supplies not readily available here." He paused. "Enough perhaps," he finally added, "to buy a miracle."

"A miracle such as the Priests of the One God pray for daily?"

"Something more practical." Janos kept his voice cautious. "A weapon unlike anything seen upon any battlefield."

"A magical weapon?" she asked, a sudden interest obvious in her tone.

"'Tis not truly magic."

"But it will seem like magic." She seemed to smiling, but the pale moonlight failed to throw enough light on her face for Janos to be certain. Moonlight did catch her ring and it sparkled brightly.

"To some it will. My display at dinner was merely the smallest flash of what my thunder dust can do." Unsure what else to say, Janos waited for what seemed to be an eternity.

Sapphire finally nodded. "I have wagered many more of my coins on gambles offering far fewer returns, friend Janos. You shall have your coins and supplies for this project."

"I thank you, my Lady. Keff and I are honored to take you on as our secondary patron."

"I will have the coins brought to your quarters within a few days. You may deliver me a proper accounting later."

"Of course." Janos bowed to her. "Thank you again, my Lady."

"Leave me now."

Bowing once again, Janos hurried from the garden.

Chapter Seven

"The latest rumours are flying about the marketplace." The merchant lifted his mug to the barmaid for a refill. "The Royal Court has issued a statement of blame for the death of Merchant Delmar."

"Let me guess the guilty parties," Janos muttered into his ale. He and Keff were seated at a nearby table, but neither merchant was taking care to avoid being overheard. Both men had apparently drunk more than was wise.

"Elves." The merchant drank deeply from his mug. "A good vintage, wench." He pinched her bottom.

"I knew it!" Janos cursed. "We get blamed for everything!"

"Shush!" Keff told him. "Maybe this is only a rumour."

"'Tis said that a coven of sorcerers sought to cast the Dark Arts upon the city and were destroyed by their own miscast spell."

"Good riddance to them." The merchant's companion spat onto the sawdust-covered floor. "A pity the curse did not slay all their kind."

"Aye."

Janos looked around the tavern glumly. The crowd was the usual eclectic mixture. Merchants and off-duty Guardsmen. White-robed Priests of the One God. Shopkeepers and travelers. Rich men and poor. "Human and Elf drinking in companionship...as long as none know the truth of their comrade's bloodlines."

"Don't fret yourself, Janos. No one knows you're a Half-Blood."

"Thank you for reminding me." Janos stood up. "I'll see you at home."

"What did I say?" Keff asked, surprised.

Janos stepped into the street and drew his cloak more tightly around his thin torso. The night air was cool against his face. He looked up at the moon. "Ye Gods!" he said aloud. "Why do you test your children so?"

The Gods, as usual, did not answer.

* * *

"This struck me as a good time to talk, Janos." Sapphire stood by the workshop door. "The night is young and the household is relaxing." She wore a pale green gown, with gold embroidery at the hem and neck.

"Our master is not present then?"

"No, he gone to the moon-quarter devotions at the Temple."

Startled, Janos glanced at his patroness. "He worships the One God?" he asked. *I thought he worshipped only money.*

"He goes to the Temple like all good Imperial citizens." Sapphire shrugged, and then adjusted her shawl. "If it makes him happy, then I say let him have his fun."

"You do not believe?"

"Not in the Priesthood, no. One God to rule all of Creation?" she scoffed. "How absurd. My people have long worshipped the many gods."

"The old religion."

"Aye," she agreed. "The old religion of the Elf-Kind. I am of Elf-Blood...why should I not worship the gods and goddesses of my ancestors?"

"I can see no reason."

"My brother calls the old religion wasteful and out-dated. 'The old gods are dead,' he has told me on more than one occasion."

"As did my former teacher. But you don't believe him?"

"I can feel Their presence in my heart," she replied honestly. "The Light Bearers still speak to me in my dreams...do They not whisper to you?"

"Yes," he admitted. "But not as often or in as much detail as I might wish."

"They are Gods...Their intentions towards us are mysterious."

"I wonder at their paths." Janos turned away from the candle's flame. "Why did They abandon our ancestors to the Humans all those centuries ago? Why will They allow this city to fall to the Horde?"

"Who can know the mind of a God?"

"I would like to. I feel like a piece on a gaming board...though often I do not know the rules or even the game I am supposedly playing."

"My brother used to question everything...I often think that is one of the reasons he turned away from the old ways and gave his allegiance to the One God."

"The Priesthood claim easy answers."

"But they can offer few miracles to demonstrate their One God's existence."

"The Emperor seems convinced."

"The Emperor is old and dying." Sapphire sighed. "The One God is what the Empire worships publicly. And my brother is far from the only one willing to turn his back on the old ways."

"I had noticed his eagerness for embracing Imperial law and custom."

"My brother concerns himself overmuch with the doings of the Court and the Families. I prefer to spend my time in more scholarly pursuits."

"I had not noticed, my Lady."

Sapphire smiled. "You are observant enough in your ways that I think you cannot help but see the scope of my interests." She rested her hand on a crystal sphere. "He sees the old blood as a taint."

Janos smiled at her. "Whereas we see it to be—"

"An advantage, I dare think." She smiled.

"A small one at best."

"After so long, how many family bloodlines are still pure?" Sapphire asked him plainly. "Intermarriage between us, the offspring of centuries, past rapes long-forgotten...who can now tell which of the Noble Families are truly completely free of Elf-blood?"

"Very few, I would think."

"Very few indeed. And those that are pure...or nearly pure have the potential to change everything."

"I doubt even the Imperial Family are still as pure as they would have the rest of us believe."

"I am not confining my observations merely to humankind, friend Janos. The purity of Elf-blood is also important to track."

Janos shrugged. "I fear mostly only by the Priesthood of the One God and the Imperial Court. The common folk care little for the blood flowing in one's veins. They care only to spill it."

* * *

"By order of his Imperial Majesty, Valorium the Venerable, these new soldiers of the Guard are sworn into service. Loyalty to the Crown. Duty unto death." The captain lowered his scroll. "March!" he bellowed.

Janos and Keff stood watching the line of newly commissioned Guards march out of the square. "Will they be enough?'

"Those conscripts?" Mica snorted, then swore under his breath. "Farmers and shepherds mostly among the volunteers. Beggars, vagrants, men unlucky enough to stumble into a press gang...those are the fine defenders of the Guard. The Emperor is desperate enough to seize up whomever he can to press into his army." He eyed the lines of marching soldiers. "They might slow the Horde down if they can trip more of them than themselves. Otherwise the Horde will be at our walls ere winter."

Janos closed his eyes.

Keff shrugged. "At least the riots will settle." Many of the recent rioters had been arrested and conscripted into the Guards.

"For now."

A trio of priests in gleaming white robes strode along the street, the crowds parting before them. "The blessings of the One be upon you," the oldest intoned to a shopkeeper.

The man bowed deeply. "How may I serve?"

"Your finest cloth," the priest said. "In the purest of white, of course, so that all might see the radiance of the One reflecting from our garments as we walk in his glory."

"Listen to that drivel," Keff muttered. "Does anyone actually take them seriously?'

"The Emperor does. And so does most of the Court."

"No one important then."

Janos gave his companion a look.

"I must get back to my duties," Mica announced. "Before I have to arrest you for treason and dissent against the Emperor."

Keff snickered. "If you arrest me, I'll have to denounce you."

"Denounce me?"

"Yeah. I saw the scrolls you tried to keep hidden under your pillow."

"What were *you* doing in his bedchamber?" Janos demanded.

"That is what I want to know too." Mica rested his hand on his sword.

"I was looking for the lavatorium?"

"The privy is out back...where it has always been."

"Good thing you told me." Keff smiled and waved. "Must dash." He hurried away down the street.

Mica looked at Janos with a sigh of exasperation. "He never grows up, does he?"

"Not that I have observed."

* * *

Janos took another sip of his wine and winced at the taste. It had a bitter bite, but then *The Sour Grapes* was not known for the treasures of its cellars. He was reading a scroll, keeping his face hidden behind it while he awaited the arrival of a compatriot.

"So did you hear about the small riot in the lesser market?" The voice bore the accent of the western lands.

"Aye, but only that one had occurred. What have you heard?"

"'Twas a witch that sparked it. Half-blood bitch, of course. Tried to cast a spell within the market and enraged the crowd. Proper God-fearing souls that they were, they chased her from their midst."

Janos peered over the top of his scroll. Two outlander merchants, from their garb. *The tavern manages a brisk business*, he noted dryly.

The merchant on the left raised his mug to his lips. "Did the Guard take her for questioning?"

"No, she was torn limb-from-limb before the Guard could intervene." The other man laughed and lifted his wine to his lips to finish it.

Keeping his face hidden behind his scroll, Janos sighed and shook his head. A most likely innocent woman torn apart by a mob simply because she was a half-blood. *Such is the state of things within the Empire.*

"Master?"

Janos lowered the scroll. "Yes?" His tongue stopped working as he stared at the vision before him.

The blonde-haired woman offered him a nod. "You look lonely." She had piercing blue eyes, having no doubt used a touch of powder to make them stand out even more. The slight tilt to her eyes betrayed the Elf-blood in her veins.

Janos licked his lips. She was young, but had a body that would have made any of the goddesses envious. "No, I'm waiting for someone."

She sat down. "You have found someone, silly." She offered him a warm smile and placed her hand on his arm. "You can call me Amber."

"And what a pretty bauble you are." The speaker was a tall man, broad-shouldered, with a thick black beard. "Why don't you come back to my quarters for the night?"

"All right. This one doesn't seem interested in my company." She rose, stretching out her arms and her back—which did amazing things with her bosom. "Perhaps he would prefer to visit with the Eunuchs." With a last, lingering look, Amber turned and swayed her way out of the common-room.

Janos felt a tinge of regret at her departure. *She would be worth every coin in my purse*, he thought. Then he cursed himself. *The best she can do with her life is to be a courtesan. How low have* my *people truly fallen?*

He lifted his arm to signal the waitress for another drink and something clinked onto the wine-stained tabletop. He looked down in surprise. Golden candlelight glinted from the face of small silver token.

Janos picked it up and studied it closely. "What is this?" he wondered aloud. *A coin?* It was not one of the Empire's crowns. He looked at it more closely. There was an emblem on it. *A star or a stylized sun?* It had a hole bored through near what he assumed to be the top edge. "A medallion?" He stuffed the coin into his purse and sighed. *Where is he?* Warren was late...very late.

Chapter Eight

"Perhaps we need to consult with someone more versed in the ancient arts than ourselves."

"We tried that. Warren failed to make our meeting. I drank three mugs of foul wine in *The Sour Grapes* and have nothing to show for my evening there."

"Nothing save a bad case of wine-head?"

"Yes, aside from that." Luckily he had a stash of medicinal herbs to deal with such ills. "It took a not inconsiderable amount of pounding at the door to get that dratted warden to open it for me."

"He was no doubt asleep."

"You were snoring."

Keff snickered. "I knew enough to go to bed at a decent hour."

"You never did when we worked for Anton."

"You had your share of late nights too."

"I know." Janos sighed and gave an idle tug at the medallion Amber had left him. He had strung a slender leather cord through the hole and hung it around his neck. "We need access to the old knowledge."

"Like the ancients had?" Keff snickered. "I doubt that Master Colm would be pleased to hear that we're conducting a spirit-calling inside his house."

"Don't even joke about such things!" Janos shivered as a sudden gust of wind howled outside the shuttered window. "The dead are nothing to joke about."

"My people don't fear the dead."

"You Hillmen don't fear anything."

"And Elf-kind fear anything dead."

"The Elves revere life. When the spirit departs this plane, it should not be recalled."

"Which brings us full circle. We need more information about the mixing of thunder dust. The ancients must have had something similar."

Keff picked up a small scroll. "The legend of Torenth Hammerhand says that the Elf mages of Castille Radiance 'hurled their lightnings to rend the ground beneath his army'. Sounds like a thunder dust to me."

"Perhaps. It could just be a legend."

"I would suggest that you visit the Library." Sapphire smiled at their surprise as she emerged from the shadows.

"Apologies, my Lady. We did not hear you enter." Janos glanced at the workshop's door. *I would have sworn to the all the Gods that I had locked it.*

"I was passing by and noticed your candles. I had thought to check on your work's progress."

"So far, we have not much to report." Keff shrugged. "We're having trouble finding the right mixture of chemicals. Our master's records were not as accurate as we had hoped."

"Or else we lost the right scrolls during the fire."

"That too."

Janos sighed loudly and smoothed out his tunic. "There are far too many changes to check if we are to discover the correct proportions to achieve a potent and safe mixture."

"If we get it right, we'll have a weapon that can crush the Horde. If we mix it wrongly, then we'll probably blow up the very crews trying to wield it." Keff shook his head, and then chuckled grimly. "The Emperor had better hire a lot more mercenaries...and promise to pay them after the battle is won."

Sapphire also smiled briefly at the gallows's humor. "I quite understand your concerns. You are seeking to rediscover what was likely common knowledge to the ancients." She smiled again, this time her expression was more comforting. "So I would suggest a little digging in the Library." Her calm gaze drifted across Keff to focus intently upon Janos. "You might find the scrolls stored down in the lowermost levels to be most illuminating."

* * *

Janos moved through the corridors of the Library as quietly as he could. "This would have been so much easier if Warren had made our meeting," he grumbled. Room after room of scroll-laden shelves waited in dusty stillness. The Great Library of Salidaraselom was famous throughout the world. *A veritable tomb of knowledge,* he thought as he carefully and silently stepped around a pair of Temple Guardsmen standing in the aisle talking.

Most of the corridors were empty. Janos had seen a bare handful of scholars and a few priests making use of the chambers, but most of the city ignored the treasure in their midst. Even the city's normal noises were muted within the near-holy confines.

"Are you lost, Sir?"

At the soft voice, Janos froze in mid-step. "Ah…" He stared blankly at the robed librarian. "I am looking for the History Section."

"What era?" The elderly man was dressed in a gray robe that made his skin seem even more washed out. Torchlight flickered across him, throwing half a dozen shadows onto the floor and walls.

I hope they have wards against fire, Janos thought. "Pre-Imperial," he said aloud.

"Pre-Imperial?" The librarian's eyebrows lifted to where his hairline would have been if advancing age had left him any hair. "Pre-Imperial?" he repeated in a slightly louder voice.

Janos swallowed in a suddenly dry throat.

"Those sections are kept within the lower basements. Access to those scrolls is restricted by order of his Majesty." He gave Janos an appraising look.

"I am a scholar of some reputation."

"Should I have heard of you then?"

"Well," Janos began and began to brush at his tunic in a nervous gesture he had long since given up trying to break. "That is to say possibly. Depending on your interests and area of—"

"Sir, I shall have to ask you for—" the old man's voice trailed away.

Janos followed the librarian's suddenly sharp stare to his chest. Down to his gleaming medallion.

"The Luminary." The librarian's tone took on a sound of reverence as he breathed the word. "Why did you not show me that at once?" he demanded. His left hand twitched.

"I had not—"

"This way please, good Master." The now-obsequious librarian offered him a quick bow. "The full resources of this institution are at your disposal, of course. Should you require any assistance, you need only ask. My name is Jerome."

"Thank you, Jerome. Simply show me to the scrolls."

"The quickest path lies just beyond this door." Jerome took a bundle of keys from a pouch at his belt. "One cannot be too careful with certain writings," he explained as he unlocked the door. "Imperial orders and simple sense must protect the uninitiated from their baser instincts."

"I understand." The door opened onto a spiral staircase. No torches flickered in the depths.

Jerome took a torch from the wall. "This way." He began to descend the stairs.

It was a long staircase that they walked, leading Janos to wonder just how old the library truly was. *How much history has it been built over?* The basement was veritable warren of corridors and alcoves, with only a narrow pathway between stacks of crates and boxes and barrels and shelves upon shelves. *'Tis indeed a tomb.*

Holding the torch steady, Jerome led the way unerringly through half a dozen turnings until he reached another locked door. "The collected works of the Pre-Imperial era," he announced with satisfaction. "That is, what writings survived the burnings and purges of course." He sounded sad, regretting the loss of knowledge and information.

"Thank you." Janos eyed the laden shelves. "So many scrolls."

"Hundreds certainly. In this room alone." Jerome looked around and then lit a small lantern he spotted atop a desk. "They are very old."

"I'm sure they are."

"Be careful with them, Master. There is parchment and ink in that desk should you require them for note making. I can have a scribe sent down to assist you?"

"No, thank you. I will be fine on my own."

"Of course. Good luck with your research then. May the spark of knowledge illuminate your path." Jerome wandered off into the warren.

Janos eyed the scrolls. "How will I ever find what I need?" he mused.

* * *

"Jerome has been most helpful. Every time I go to the library he hastens to guide me down into the cellars. He has fresh torches lit and waiting. He even had a small pitcher of wine there the last time."

"You get *wine*?" Keff's mouth gaped. "How do you rate so highly? I get kicked out of the upper levels."

"I saw the scrolls you were trying to read," Mica reminded him in a dry tone. "Those ones *should* have been banned." He passed around the cheese platter.

"There's nothing wrong with them," Keff protested. "They portray human nature in all its glory."

"Those pictures are purely artistic imagination."

"They're still nice."

"If you two are quite finished?" Janos waited until they had fallen silent. "It was difficult, but I have at last managed to decipher some of the writings in the scrolls. But the language has changed and the spelling is simply archaic." Who would have thought that language and writing would alter so much in a few centuries?

"I have some skill in reading the old tongues. Perhaps I can translate them for you."

"Your offer is most generous, my Lady." Mica bowed to her.

Sapphire smiled and refilled his mug with wine. "We shall need to think harder, Master Feldspar."

"Indeed, my Lady."

"And you must think faster. Reports are arriving almost daily about the southward progress of the Horde. The Emperor's Guardsmen cannot slow them. The northern garrisons are collapsing."

"If the garrisons fail to hold back the Horde, then what hope has the city?"

"None, I fear." Janos pulled his cloak more tightly around himself. "I have faith in my inventions, but can we convince the City Guard to make use of them?"

Mica shook his head. "That can be my worry. Janos, all you must do is prepare your devices for testing. A public testing," he added sharply. "With a sufficiently awe-inspiring display, you can almost certainly attract attention from the Court."

"And that will save us?"

"I hope so."

Chapter Nine

"They don't look like much, nephew."

"They work more for my sister than myself."

"Yes, Uncle Galen." She offered him a smile. "These two scholars are labouring hard on the behalf of the city."

"The far-seer tubes the Guardsmen introduced? A fine toy no doubt. Ah, Sapphire, your brother indulges you too much. Sometimes I think you aspire to seek wealth and power far above your station. The allowance he grants you is more than generous enough for a lady of your refinement."

"Perhaps I do at that." Colm scowled at Janos and Keff who tried to ignore his presence. "Come, Uncle, and allow me to show you the pride of my cellars. A vintage from Ceres harvested merely ten harvests back."

"Ah, I have heard that the Ceres crop was especially good in that particular year though I have not yet had the good fortune to sample any of it myself. I had not thought that you would have some hidden away within your cellar though."

"One of my clients failed to make a timely payment. The contents of his cellars were varied and plentiful." Laughing at the misfortune of others, the two men vanished around a corner.

Sapphire watched them. "Uncle Galen was my father's brother. Pureblood, my brother envies him for obvious reasons."

"He does not know of your heritage?"

"I think not. Mother was careful not to show any untoward skills or attitudes. Nor did she reveal the extent of her personal wealth."

"A wise choice."

"If it was left to my uncle, I would be married to some pureblood lout by now...or else serving in the Temple." She shivered at the thought. "Such is not my desire."

"Tomorrow we must venture to the workshop. I have some tests to try and I would not care to conduct them here."

"I will accompany you."

"That is not necessary, my Lady."

"Ah, but it is. My brother takes a dim view of his servants leaving the confines of the house these days. He fears desertion."

"Though I can see why some might prefer never to return to these grim walls, I have seen the streets outside. Trust me, even with Colm's tender ministrations," he rubbed at his long-faded bruises, "I have no desire to be reduced to begging or trying to find another patron." The streets were not safe.

"I will mention your loyalty and devotion to my brother," Sapphire smiled, "thought I doubt he will care overmuch."

* * *

The labouratorium remained secure from the rampaging mobs and rioting citizenry.

"We're safe and sound."

"Don't be so certain."

"What?" Keff looked around. "The street's deserted."

"From the scratches and dings, someone has tried to break in, but at least the stout locks and hinges stopped them." Janos pulled a key from his belt pouch and fumbled with the lock Anton had installed years before. "I would hate to think what mischief someone could cause with the contents of my shelves."

"Our shelves."

"*Our* shelves," Janos agreed sourly.

"Oh, probably poison in the wells."

"Fire in the canals with the right chemical mixture."

"The Perfumed Quarter remains secure with its title as the worst slum in the Empire." Sapphire pulled her cloak more tightly around herself, to better hide her fine gown and its embroidery from the watching eyes of any desperate passersby. "Yet it is not without its charms." A gust of breeze brought the stink of rotting garbage to her nostrils. "Though I admit that I fail to see them as yet."

The door creaked open.

"Enter, my Lady." Janos lit a candle while Keff carefully locked the door behind them.

"That was fun."

Janos turned towards his friend. "You get too much thrill from walking the streets with that oversized dagger of yours! You're turning half-barbarian yourself."

Keff patted the short sword he had belted under his cloak. "We have to defend ourselves from footpads and thieves."

"By breaking the law and carrying arms?"

"The thieves have weapons too I might point out. We're honest men constrained by unfair laws and the evils of our fellow men."

Sapphire laughed softly. "He wears that sword well."

"No doubt your brother took it from a child. Such a blade would fit someone of Dwarf-height."

"I am Hillman, not Dwarf!"

"Of course you are."

A knock sounded from the door.

"Yes?" Janos called through it. He reached for the cover of the small spy-hole. "Who is it?"

"'Tis I—Mica."

"Come in!" Janos hastily threw open the door. "Praise the Gods. You got my note."

"Aye." Mica stepped inside and then slammed the door behind him. "I was leading a patrol and thought that my under-captain could stand some experience on his own. There's been a lot of rapid promotions recently in the ranks."

"I cannot understand why," Sapphire interjected in a dry tone of voice.

"Promising leaders are being given troops and sent out to the fight the Horde. The Emperor no doubt hopes that new blood will turn the tide where his more experience troops have failed."

"More experienced and more loyal."

"Aye. He's been recalling some of his more loyal legions to bolster the city's own Guard."

"And further repress us."

"Not necessarily. When the Horde reach the walls, every hand that can hold a weapon will likely be called to man them."

Janos shivered at the thought. "I am a scholar," he announced, "not a soldier."

"I was an aspiring scribe once," Mica told him.

Keff stared at him in surprise. "You never mentioned that before. When was this?"

"Back in the farming village of Jorpa's Girdle. My family owned over five hundred head of cattle and twice that many sheep. We had a nice estate. Rich lands and a number of men farming the land. In a good year we sent a dozen wagonloads of goods to the capitol to pay our taxes."

Keff whistled. "Sounds like a nice life."

"It was." Mica's voice turned grim. "Until the Horde came."

Janos winced.

"Two days warning was all that we had. Two days of watching the dust raised by marching men and galloping horses come ever closer. Two days to pack whatever we could, gather what herds we could, and flee south. The Imperial Guard took most of our cattle on the road and when we reached the Northern Bridge, I was conscripted into the Guards and sent back north.

"I lost my family then, in the confusion and chaos. I think they fled to Mirtoxas, but I'm not sure. I took to the soldiering life though. The food was terrible, the pay poor, and the officers worse, but it was action and a purpose that I seldom felt back on the farm. We held the Bridge for half a year. Six moons of endless waiting and then swirls of desperate battle."

Janos whistled softly. "So that's why you hardly ever talk about your life before."

"Fighting the Horde was just like trying to fight a windstorm or a grassland fire." Mica shook his head. "They would come galloping at your lines by the hundreds. Shrieking out war-cries and curses alike in their incomprehensible tongue. Leather-clad, with bows held ready. Those damned bows would tear holes through your ranks, leaving the survivors shaken and wavering. Then they'd hit you with another charge and another. By the time the main thrust came, half your troops would be dead and the rest demoralized. The key to surviving a battle, let alone dreaming about winning, was maintain the morale of your own troops. Too easy for their will to fight to be lost and then you were left with a mob being pursued and slaughtered by the Horde."

"But you survived? Obviously."

"We held the Horde at Northbridge."

"I recall that. There was much rejoicing in the streets when word came of that victory."

"Even my brother was pleased by that news," Sapphire added.

"The Horde weren't stopped by any act of the military," Mica told them bluntly. "Despite what the Court reported to you. It was no strategy, just the lay of the land in that region."

"'Tis good to be schooled in knowledge of geography."

"Aye, Janos, or at least in the logistics of moving an army. The Bridge stopped them. There were ten thousand Keli'cairn horsemen but just one bridge. We held the forts, though the northern side of the city was burned in the fighting. The Horde couldn't swim nor ride across the fast-flowing river. It was a stalemate of sparring. They would try to take the forts and we would drive them back. Our captains would send out occasional sorties to try and disrupt the Horde. They killed a few officers, but never enough to make any sort of difference.

"I was chosen to escort a convoy of the wounded here to the capitol. The Gods blessed me in that I was reassigned to the Legion of the City Guard. Otherwise I would have been sent back out to fight before I would have the had the pleasure of meeting you, my Lady."

Sapphire blushed. "You are too kind."

"So that brings us to the present," Mica finished. "And your wonderful invention, Janos."

"The thunder dust, once we get it perfected, has the potential to save the Empire," Sapphire said as she poured wine into Mica's mug.

"Aye, my Lady." Janos was momentarily struck dumb by the sight of a wealthy lady pouring wine for a mere Guardsman. "With it in our army, we could drive the barbarians back into the Waterless Wastes."

"Without it, the Empire crumbles and the city will fall."

"Aye," Janos agreed sourly. "A most perplexing puzzle. The Gods toy with us in a most dour fashion." A sudden breeze from the Bay brought the stink of rotting garbage to his nostrils. "Gah." He lit a small brazier, sprinkling the coals with dried incense. *I hate this Gods-ignored neighborhood.*

Sapphire shook her head. "A slim chance of success is all that we have left to consider. Perhaps we should flee from the city while we still are able. I still see that as our only option."

"Aye, but to where?" Mica countered. "Where can we run?"

"The eastern lands remain free from the Horde."

"Thus far, my Lady."

"Aye, thus far," she nodded. "My ancestors came from the east. We should journey there."

"To the Elves?"

"To what remains of the free lands." She smiled. "Granted my people do not command the empire they once did, but we still have some hidden cities and strongholds. Across the Bay, beyond the Sandoval Mountains, we could find safety."

"The journey will be long and tiring," Mica warned.

"And dangerous."

"It will still be a damn sight safer than staying here."

Am I a scholar or have I become a truce negotiator? Or, dare I think it, a matchmaker? "So how do we flee the city?" Janos asked the question that was uppermost in his mind. "Should we truly decide to flee, then how do we arrange it?"

"By ship," Keff burst out. "We can board a ship in the harbour."

"Have you seen the harbour lately?" Mica asked them grimly. "The Guards are maintaining a strong presence there. Ships arrive with supplies for the city and Guards are watching the grain. Every ship that sails is heavily laden with refugees fleeing the city. Noble families and wealthy merchants are buying passage. Hordes of commoners are begging for a ride just across the Bay. I know not that we could even reach a ship, let alone have enough coin to buy passage."

"My brother has half a dozen ships crossing the Bay as fast as the galley slaves can row. He is making a fine profit with the ferry trade."

"Could we take advantage of that?"

"I doubt it. How would you reach one of his ships through the mob?"

"What about by fleeing by land?" Keff asked.

"That is more likely. But what of the Horde? We have walls, not the endless grasslands to defend us now."

"The Horde will besiege the walls." Mica gestured to the map they had spread across the table top. "I saw them do such beyond the Gap. I saw it in person and heard tales from other soldiers. They lay siege for as long as it takes. They starve a city into submission. Wait for disease and famine to take its toll. And they don't just wait for the defenders to lose heart. They launch assault after assault with their endless numbers. Batter down the gates. Scale the walls. Whatever it takes."

"Can we hold?"

"The Guards will fight," Mica vowed, "for the Emperor has vowed that Salidaralesom will stand unto the Last Days."

"But *can* we hold?" Keff repeated.

Mica shook his head sadly. "I do not think so."

Sapphire refilled her mug. "You do not?'

Mica shook his head. "The Horde is simply too vast, their numbers too strong. They have taken every city and town north of the Gap. They *are* taking every city and town south of the Gap. Salidaralesom is be the last of the great cities to lay in their path...and it will be the last of the great cities to fall."

Part Two: Lighting The Fuse

Chapter Ten

"Stand present and listen to these, the words of his Imperial Majesty!" The herald was wearing a dark blue cloak over his lighter blue tunic. He unrolled a scroll and cleared his throat. "By direct order of his Imperial Majesty, Valorium the Venerable, the noble Gabrielle Thorn is hereby declared traitor. Her lands and title are now forfeit. Let her bloodline be stricken from the Court and let every hand be turned against her. May she be hunted without food or rest until she dead and crumbled into dust."

"What did she do?" Janos asked, as the marketplace remained silent.

A merchant turned and glanced at him. "The bitch declared Mirtoxas an independent city-state."

Keff whistled.

"Her troops have already taken the Transcendent Bridge across the Whitewater and secured the bridge forts." Mica kept his voice low as he joined his friends. "The Emperor lacks the troops to storm the bridge forts." The Empire's far-flung garrisons had been stripped bare to supply troops to fight the Horde.

"And so she's got her own realm." High cliffs lined the Whitewater for much of the river's length south of the mountains, and many stretches contained fierce rapids and were thus impassible to boats. "The Bridge was the only way to cross for leagues and leagues."

"Aye...she has the perfect defence against the Horde." Burn down the bridge and no one could cross. "She holds the forts on this shore, though the Emperor's loyalists lay siege to them. Most of the Toraxis town has burned in the fighting."

"Ye Gods, how can the nobility be so stupid? They bicker and fight amongst themselves while the Horde descends on their holdings."

"Only united can we hope to hold and we are fare from united." Janos shook his head. "The Horde will triumph and nothing we can do will stop it." Even the promise of the thunder dust seemed a frail shield against the nightmares that would plague him this night.

"I suggest that you and your patroness begin to pack. Quietly, mind and don't let the Vulture know."

"Pack?"

"Yes, gather up what you deem most valuable and hide them someplace easy to grab if you must flee the house."

"Do you think things are truly that bad?"

"I know they are. The rioting will be worse ere the Horde reaches the walls. The Vulture is not loved by his neighbours and rumours of his supposed wealth have spread throughout the city. That house will be the centre of a riot someday and sooner rather than later." He gave his head a shake. "Pack, Janos, and be ready to flee at a moment's notice."

* * *

"What word from the Court?"

"Nothing yet I fear." Sapphire stood on the balcony, a pale white cloak draped over her silver dress. "Just the smoke still rising."

"More smoke?" Janos stepped onto the patio. "Are there more fires breaking out?" he moved closer to the parapet.

"The rioting has not abated from yesterday."

"Where is the City Guard?"

"Probably in the middle of the rioting." Sapphire's voice held a note of concern as she stared into the twilight. "There are numerous fires near the Guards' barracks."

"Mica has his own home," Janos told her quickly. "I don't see any smoke rising near his street."

"Oh, thank the Gods." Her cheeks coloured. "He has become a friend and I would not wish him harm in such chaos."

"Of course not, my Lady," Janos agreed. *Just friends?*

"He is a Guardsman and thus is drawn into danger." She gripped the edge of the wall with white-knuckles. "He is too brave to run from danger."

"Aye, he is brave. But, I do not think he is eager to throw his life away in the defence of this city. Not any longer."

"Do you truly believe that?" she asked. "Oh, hold a moment. My uncle has just returned from the Citadel." She could gaze down into the courtyard below. "He seems worried. And the worse for drink."

Janos stepped forward, stepping up to her side.

"What news?" Colm demanded as he strode out of his house and into the courtyard. He was clutching at a stout wooden staff, though whether to support his bulk or for protection from unseen foes was not certain. "What word do you bring us?"

"'Tis chaos up there." The older man's voice carried well. He was clutching a wine flask in his hand and he hastily drank from it. "The Court is in anarchy. Half the nobles are fighting with the others. One faction wishes to open negotiations and make terms with the Horde."

"I'd sooner die!"

"So would the other faction. Hence the varied confusion. The Priesthood is seeking to garner more power and influence for itself, with varying degrees of success. The Guardsmen are being given inconsistent orders. March there. Stand down. Arrest this lord or that noble."

"This is what comes of half-bloods taking power unto themselves."

"But where is the Emperor?" Janos asked quietly. "Why doesn't he do something?"

Sapphire shrugged helplessly. "I cannot say."

Colm must have asked something similar for Galen answered loudly. "They say that he is ill. Or else dead."

"Civil war or else a war of succession...either will cripple our city's defences at the very moment when they must be the most strong."

"Aye, nephew. Now, have you anymore of the Ceres hidden within your cellar? I would taste the sweet nectar of such rare grapes again ere the city falls."

"Indeed, Uncle. Come this way."

"By the Gods," Janos whispered. "By all the Blessed Gods." He staggered away from the balcony's edge. "The city is truly doomed now. Thunder dust or not, we cannot hope to stand against the Horde when our own rulers cannot be stopped from infighting."

"Then I fear we shall be turning to our alternate plan." The lady's fingers tightened on the railing. "We shall flee the city and seek our safety elsewhere."

Janos turned to stare across the rooftops towards the citadel. "It's burning!" he gasped. Flames were crackling and rising above one portion of the graceful battlements. "'Tis civil war."

Sapphire stared at the rising column of smoke. "Mica will be up there." The ruby on her finger sparkled.

* * *

"And make certain that the door is kept barricaded at all times." Colm waddled along the corridor, issuing a string of sharp commands to his secretary who copied down notes. "Have the new watchmen loaned to us from my uncle bed down in one of those old storerooms."

"Of course, my Lord."

"Problems, Brother?"

"Yes, constant ones, Sister." Colm shook his head at her as she stepped out of a cross corridor with Janos and Keff in tow behind her. "Imperial order has broken down completely I fear. Fighting between factions of various nobles has broken out in the streets...and the rioters are turning on anyone they please."

"Mostly on the Half bloods, yes?"

"Yes. The Half bloods are likely the ones responsible for the chaos out there. I tell you, most of those scum would be glad—*glad*!—to see the Horde take the city." Colm glared at Janos. "Luckily the Guardsmen are labouring mightily to restore order to the city. The ones responsible will be executed. The Emperor be praised." He waddled on his way, issuing more orders to prepare his house for a siege.

"Of course we remain their preferred targets for persecution." Janos sighed at the bitterness in his voice. "I'm sure that some of us are rioting against the purebloods as well. Blood is flowing out in the streets."

"Things cannot go on in this manner."

"No, of course they can't."

"The city will be a mere shell before the Horde arrive...they will shatter it without effort." Sapphire sighed. "And there is nothing that can be done."

* * *

Night-time had fallen but the city was not quiet. A dull roar rose from beyond the house's walls...a wordless growl from a hundred throats.

"Another riot."

"How can it be *another* riot?" Keff asked as he tied a sack to the mule. I don't think the one from last week has ended yet."

"We must make our final plans to depart soon." Sapphire was dressed in a simple red gown with a light grey cloak draped over her shoulders; she did not look like a woman of wealth. "The riots are spreading as quickly as the fires. This house will be a target for many."

"The rumoured treasure." If Colm did possess such treasure as street-rumour claimed, Janos had yet to see it. *And I have searched through most of this house on pretext or another by now.*

"There is the rumour of treasure and general ill-will against my brother for his business practices. Our watchmen cannot, or will not, stand up against a determined mob. Despite my Uncle's promises to the contrary. And I cannot protect us all."

"I have never wished so hard for Imperial Guardsmen to actually be out patrolling the streets."

"But they aren't." Janos shook his head. "Still no word of Mica?"

"Nothing about him specifically," Sapphire told them sadly. "Many rumours are flying though. Some of the Guardsmen *are* trying to restore order to the city. Others are supporting one faction or another in trying for the throne."

"Gods." Janos shook his head.

"At least we listened and had our packs ready for this night."

"I did not think it would come so soon, Keff." Janos turned his head. Sapphire was standing near the stable door, staring at her house. "Will your brother join our flight?"

"Nay," she shook her head sadly, "he will not flee. He and Uncle Galen have barricaded the main doors and vowed to hold this house against rioters and Keli'cairn alike." She smiled. "I think they stand a fair chance of doing so." She turned to check on the mule. "Several of my likeminded relatives have flocked to this house with provisions and weapons and retainers."

"Prepared for a siege?"

"Yes. They will stay here until the end."

"My Lady, are you certain you will accompany us?"

"Yes, Janos, I will not stay here. Salidaralesom will fall. The Horde close in around us and I feel their hands at my throat. I will seek solace and safety beyond the walls." Her lips twitched in a smile as the Temple bell tolled mournfully.

Chapter Eleven

A dull thud echoed through the night-darkened courtyard.

"A battering ram?"

"Yes. The rioting has reached this neighborhood." Sapphire listened quietly. The noise that was the voice of the mob had been growing louder for hours.

"Where is the Guard?"

"Keff, that mob probably *is* the Guard."

Sapphire sighed loudly. "It has come to this."

"Murder in the night."

Colm's voice rose from within the house in an angry shout.

"Then let us go now." Sapphire led them into the garden. "We can leave unseen through here." She pulled some of the vines aside, seeking something in the wall itself. "Ah, here it is."

Janos blinked at the hidden doorway. "I had no idea that portal was there."

"Of course not," the lady replied with a hint of a smile. "A secret exit cannot truly be secret if everyone knows where it can be found."

The portal opened onto one of the city's canals. A narrow pathway separated the canal from the garden wall.

Keff pulled the mule through the opening, cursing the beast as it proved reluctant to move. With the sound of his voice to prod it, it finally followed him.

Janos stepped through next. "Another patron abandoned," he mused aloud. "Another flight into a foul-smelling alley."

"At least this time we have our gear with us."

Sapphire turned back to the small gate and pulled it closed behind her. She locked it carefully and then threw the key into the canal. "I will not make it easy for any to harm my family," she explained as the splash echoed.

"Of course not, my Lady."

The three hurried along the path to where it rejoined the main street.

"The Gods favour us."

"For now." The bulk of the rioters seemed to be concentrating at the front of the house.

Shouts of anger and rage echoed from beyond the wall. Colm's voice was loudest among them, cursing those who would threaten him.

"I'm going to miss the old Vulture," Keff commented as they hurried across the Topaz Bridge.

Janos noticed that Sapphire had slowed her pace and was standing alongside the mule. "We must hurry," he said gently. "This is no place for us to linger." There was no one else in sight, but he did not trust the streets to remain empty. *Mobs, footpads, Guardsmen alike...no one is safe to meet this night.*

"I know." Sapphire looked back at the wall of her brother's house. "Fare thee well," she said softly. "May the Light Bearers shelter you."

Keff rested his hand on his sheathed dagger. "Do you think we will be safe?" he asked the others.

"Of course." Janos tried to fill his voice with a confidence he did not feel. "Come, we must hurry."

Sapphire gave the reins a tug.

"I hope the labouratorium is well locked."

"I locked it myself, Keff."

"And I have placed it under my protection." Moonlight glinted from Sapphire's ring. "I have some skill in these matters."

Janos shivered.

* * *

It was a slow and nerve-wracking journey across the chaos-stricken city. Janos lost count of the number of times that he and his companions sought shelter down alleys and huddled inside alcoves as mobs of looters and rioters passed by. Flickers of torchlight and the shouts of voices were often their only warning. Screams of fear and pain echoed across the city. The clash of weapons and the shouts of men also filled the air.

"We're going too far out of our path," Keff complained. "We should not have come anywhere near the Bridge of Pearls."

"We had to travel farther east," Janos replied. "You heard the fighting down the Bellmakers' Street." They had to detour past the crowds.

"And the fires raging in the Bootmakers' Street," Sapphire replied. Oddly, she sounded almost exhilarated by the night's adventure.

Janos studiously ignored a crumpled body half-buried under a mound of trash. "The city is dying around us." A handful of other seemingly innocent travelers were abroad this night. Cloaked, they moved from safe shadow to shadow in quick runs. *Maybe they aren't so innocent.*

"The Bridge Of Adoration. One of the nicer sights in this city." Sapphire's steps slowed. "Oh, to see it in the daylight. The carvings are most exquisite. A true wonder to behold."

"We don't have time for looking at artwork right now."

"The fires at the Citadel seem to dying down." The reddish glow in the sky was slowly fading.

"Someone must have restored some semblance of order up there."

"We can only hope." *More likely the flames ran out of fuel to burn.*

"I wonder if Mica is safe?"

"I know not, my Lady." Janos frowned as a figure ran past the base of the bridge.

"Keep moving," Keff hissed.

"What? Oh, of course." Janos took a stumbling step. *Was that Amber?* he wondered.

They hurried along yet another street.

Keff suddenly froze in mid-step. "Hide!"

"Where?" Janos hissed back at him. He could the tramp of booted feet. *Too many feet.*

"There!" Sapphire pointed to a small doorway.

"That won't work." Janos stepped into the shadowy alcove. "They'll see us."

"We *will* be safe," Sapphire told him in a calm voice. "Trust to the Gods."

Keff gripped his now-drawn dagger.

Janos closed his eyes and prayed silently.

A squad of Guardsmen rounded the corner with a jingle of amour. They moved past the cowering escapees without seeing them.

"That was too close."

"Neither Guards nor rioters are safe to meet tonight." Sapphire seemed unperturbed by the closeness of the encounter. "Shall we continue?" she asked, smoothing out her gown.

"Do you truly think to find safety within these walls?"

Janos whirled around, dagger drawn and ready. "Jerome!" he exclaimed.

The old man was dressed in his habitual gray robes. "The library is closed for the duration of the current crisis. So I chose to take a little sojourn through the streets. I have not left the library's confines in years and years." He sounded sad, even a little bewildered by the chaos in the city. "Have you seen the harbour recently?" he asked.

"No, we haven't." Janos stared at the dagger in his hand. "Ye Gods, what have we become?" He sheathed the blade and then hastily pulled his hand away. He pulled Jerome into motion. "We must hurry."

"Ah, the labouratorium." Janos hurried to the closed door. "Looks like someone else has tried to force the lock, but they were foiled again." He pulled out his key.

"Good workmanship on it," Keff replied. "Good fortune to us then."

"The Gods favour us." Sapphire held the mule's reins. "But I would suggest that we not tarry overmuch outside." She looked over her shoulder. "I can hear singing." Her cloak flapped in a sudden gust of breeze.

Drunken singing. Janos fumbled once more with the lock. "I hope it's not jammed," he muttered. Then it finally clicked. "Hurry!" he called as he pushed the door open. "We're safe."

* * *

"So, if we must flee the city, then how do we manage it?"

"The harbour is useless to you." Jerome kept his voice calm, though his eyes bore a haunted light. "You will never reach a ship in that mess. It is pure chaos there...hordes of panicked citizens begging for passage aboard the handful of ships. Grim-faced soldiers trying to maintain order...or else pillaging whatever they can steal."

"So we must flee by land."

"By flying over the walls?" Janos asked pointedly as he brushed lint from his sleeve. "Or do we go to the city gates and knock? Then, assuming the wardens allow us to leave, do we then politely ask the Horde not to molest us?"

"We can't out-run those horsemen. Mica told us that. Once they surround the City's walls, we'll be truly trapped."

"And the chaos that's gripping the city right now will be nothing compared to what will take over then."

"There might be another way."

"Oh?" Janos turned to face Sapphire.

She was sitting quietly in the corner. "If we cannot go *through* the wall, then perhaps we can travel under them?"

"*Under?*" Janos scratched at his head. "Perhaps the sewers might be large enough for us to crawl through." He shuddered at the thought of venturing into those dank confines. "But we will never be able to lead a mule through there. We'll be limited to what few supplies we can carry on our backs."

Sapphire smiled. "I do not think we will be reduced to crawling through the city sewers."

* * *

Thumps echoed through the shop.

"It's another mob."

"The door will hold, aye?" Jerome asked nervously. He had slept little that previous night.

"I hope it will." Keff had slept as little as Jerome.

The thumping grew louder.

"The louts must have a battering ram."

"Or a stout table."

"Ye Gods!" Jerome groaned. "We'll be slain in our beds."

"I'd prefer to die on my feet," Keff told them as the thudding continued. He was gripping his dagger.

"I'd prefer not to die at all," Janos countered. His eyes scanned the room, pondering what else could be used to the further barricade the door. "Can we not throw stuff upon them from the windows?"

"Such as?"

"Boiling oils?" Janos looked around his labouratorium and hastily catalogued its varied contents. "Surely we must have something unpleasant to cast down."

"Thunder dust."

"Not that!" Janos snapped. "We'd be likely to blow ourselves up as well as the mob."

"Go away!" Sapphire shouted through the window.

"Let us in!" one of the toughs outside called back as the battering continued to shake the door.

"We can have some fun."

"We can party."

"Begone!" Keff dumped a bucket of some foul-smelling concoction down onto them from the upstairs window.

Curses were hurled back from the mob. There were a moments of silence and the pounding at the door resumed with renewed vigour.

"What was that?" Janos puffed as he took aim with his own kettle.

"The chamber pot."

"Ew." Janos upended his kettle. More curses rose in reply as the foul liquid splashed down.

"There's too many of them!" Jerome complained as he climbed up the stairs from the ground floor.

"Then pray that the door continues to hold."

Keff nodded. "We need more things to throw down."

"Ho, the Guard!" Janos shouted. *Maybe I can trick them!* "Ho, the Guard!"

"Captain Mica! Captain Mica!" Keff shouted eagerly, thinking that Janos had actually seen an Imperial patrol and was hoping to tell the Guards who their friends were. "Captain?"

"The Gods strike thee down!" Sapphire shouted.

A cry responded.

"That sounded like someone dying." Janos froze as a second cry sounded. "My Lady?" Did she truly possess such power? Nervously, he looked through the window as the roar of the mob turned to cries of fear.

Resplendent in his armour, Mica faced off against the rapidly shrinking mob. He swung his sword in a sweeping arc and the blade sliced through a tough's club. "Go!" he shouted and the tough ran.

Janos threw open the door and Mica turned with a smile.

"Thank the Gods for your arrival!" Sapphire exclaimed.

"Thank *you* for this sword." Mica gave his blade a playful swing. "Never have I seen its like."

"I thought that blade was new." Keff gave it another look. "It looks too nice for standard issue. It's a noble's blade."

"You gave it to him?" Janos asked his patroness.

She nodded, her sharp eyes carefully studying Mica for evidence of any wounds. "My brother has had it rusting away in one of his storerooms for nearly ten winters now. He no doubt forgot about its existence long ago. He certainly did not take notice when I borrowed it to loan to a *friend*." Her tone was light. "I doubt he will worry now."

"I should thank the old vulture if I ever see him again." Mica gave them a shrug. "We should go inside before they gather their shattered courage and come back with more friends. Your door will hold up forever against such pounding."

"Are you certain?"

"Aye." Mica watched Janos lock the door again, and then cajole Keff into helping drag a heavy chest in front of the door.

"We were thinking of fleeing."

"What? Now? By daylight?"

"Well, given the mobs...."

"The streets are not safe to travel by daylight. Nor by night for that matter," Mica added.

"Even for a Guard?"

"Even for a Guards-Captain."

"We cannot hide here forever."

"No...."

"We must flee the city," Sapphire told him. "I know of long hidden tunnels which will carry us under the city walls and into the countryside."

Mica frowned. "A hidden escape tunnel? 'Tis something from a minstrel's song."

"Nonetheless, there is one."

"And you mean to use it?'

"As soon as we can reach it."

"Good thinking. We go tonight. One day's rest and then we must flee the city."

"Keff, check on the damned mule!"

Chapter Twelve

A dozen men of the Temple Guard marched past the mouth of the alley. Polished mail sparkled in the light of the torches they carried and their white cloaks shone. Not a single eyed turned to look into the shadowed depths of the alley.

Mica took his hand off his sword. He wore his breastplate and cloak, though he abandoned his leather skirt for breeches. "That was too close for comfort."

"It was." Keff shivered and drew his cloak more tightly around him.

"We must hurry." Sapphire kept her voice calm. "I would like to reach the tunnel ere morning's light reveals us to the city."

"I think the city has more important things on its collective mind than a handful of refugees." Janos winced as he trod on something that squished under foot and gave off unpleasant odours.

The dull roar of a distant riot disturbed the night.

* * *

"We have arrived."

"This is no time for shopping." Keff gestured to the locked doors in exasperation. "Even if you desperately need a new dress, the shopkeeper won't be here for hours."

Sapphire ignored him. "It should be in the basement," she said softly.

"The basement? What is in the basement?"

"The means of our escape, of course. One cannot have a secret tunnel opening onto the public street." Sapphire moved towards the rear of the building. "Coming?"

"The door is locked."

"It's only a small door. Maybe Keff and I can break it down."

"No need to damage anything, Mica. I have a key." She was moving her hand near the rusted door handle. "Everything is under control." The door slowly opened with a creak that made everyone wince. "Just down these stairs."

"How do we drag the mule down those stairs?"

"They're wide stairs."

Janos lit a torch he had taken from the mule's harness. He held it over his head. "Where is this tunnel?" he asked. The basement was most likely a storage chamber of some kind. The dirt floor bore the imprint of many booted feet and a few scraps of wood from broken crates or barrels. The walls were lined with plain wood panels. "It's very empty."

"Maybe we need to dig," Keff suggested. "Who has a shovel?"

"Not me," Mica replied as he watched Sapphire circle the room. "I doubt my sword will avail us much."

"Ah...right here."

The wooden panel swung open. "See?"

"The catacombs," Jerome sighed happily. "Here we shall make our escape."

"A hidden tunnel?"

"Aye. Surely you did not think that we should truly flee through the sewers?"

"Why did you not speak of this plan before?"

"Because I did not know if it was feasible, Janos."

"A secret tunnel...'tis like something from a child's story."

"Perhaps, Mica...but it is our best hope of making good our escape."

Keff nodded. "You speak the truth, my Lady."

"I had hoped that the tunnels were still here."

"Tunnels?" Mica stared into the darkness. "I have never heard of their existence."

"The catacombs were never common knowledge to mere humans. The first Emperor built what he planned to become his capitol city overtop the ruins of our capitol once he had overrun our ancient realm." She lit a torch. "Most of the catacombs were sealed after my people fled from these lands. Others collapsed naturally."

"*Collapsed*?"

She shrugged. "They *do* predate the Empire. It has been centuries since any maintenance or work was done upon them. Of course the timbers decay and they collapse. That said, I believe we should be able to find at least one route out of the city still passable."

Janos and Keff exchanged looks.

"Lead on then, my Lady." Mica gestured. "I shall follow as you lead and be your sword arm to protect you."

"We should not require your sword in the tunnels. If we do, then matters will truly be dire."

* * *

The tunnels were low and often choked with fallen rock.

"I hope that we will be safe."

"The Light Bearers will illuminate our path," Jerome intoned.

"As will our torches," Keff added.

"Do you have a map or something?" Janos asked.

Sapphire shook her head. "There are no maps of the catacombs."

"None to my knowledge either," Jerome added. "The library would have contained copies and I knew of none."

"I see."

"I don't like the air down here."

"'Tis stale."

"We are underground. There are no breezes until we return to the surface." Sapphire strode along without hesitation. "We should be nearing the city's outer wall by now. Soon we will begin to head upwards."

"I was not meant to be a worm," Keff grumbled.

"You're a Hillman. You should be used to tunnels."

"We are miners true," the young man agreed, "but I'm not a Dwarf!"

"I know that." Janos grinned. "You can't grow a decent beard."

"Neither can you," Keff growled back as rats scurried past them.

"Those are big rats."

The ground trembled.

"Quake!"

"Not now!" Keff cried out.

"Hold the mule!" Janos shouted back.

Rocks rained down on them and dust swirled around them.

Janos coughed and almost dropped his torch. "Why do the Gods torment us so?"

Mica was holding Sapphire in his arms.

"I'm all right," she said. "Where is Jerome?"

There was no sign of the librarian.

Just a tunnel choked with fallen rock.

Sapphire closed her eyes for a moment. "Poor Jerome."

"Perhaps he survived the fall and is on the other side."

"Then he is trapped within the city."

"A lesser fate than being crushed."

"But still a grim one."

"We cannot help him," Mica told her. "We cannot shift so much rock. Even if we knew him to be alive."

"I know...but I feel for him regardless. I led him here."

"He came willingly. You cannot blame yourself."

"Keff is right. You warned us the tunnels were unstable. It was just an accident. The will of the Gods."

Sapphire looked at him and finally nodded. "Yes, you're right." She brushed dust from her face. "We must go."

* * *

Pine trees filled their air with their scent.

"So bright, so glorious!" Janos inhaled deeply as he stumbled out of the tunnel mouth and into the daylight. "I have never liked the underground. I like it even less now."

"'Tis no place for men to be." Mica rested his hand on his sheathed sword. "Is it safe?" The land was rolling hills, mostly covered with pines and low shrubs. He saw no signs of cook-fire smoke nor traces of habitation.

"It looks that way."

Sapphire giggled. "There is very likely no one with a league of this clearing."

The mouth of the tunnel was half-choked with moss-covered boulders and further hidden by shrubs.

"I suspect that you are right about that." Janos heard nothing save the call of birds.

"I've been in worse places," Keff commented.

"Remind me not to visit the holdings of your kinfolk then," Mica grumbled.

Janos thought he could hear a faint noise. "What is that?" he asked.

"Sounds like the Bell of Invocation."

"It likely is." Sapphire adjusted her cloak. "Come, there should be a cave nearby where we can spend the night. It will be dark soon and we shall need someplace sheltered for our fire." She led Mica into the woods.

Janos and Keff exchanged glances, then followed with the mule.

Chapter Thirteen

"So now that we have escaped the city, now what?" Janos added more wood to the small fire. "The Horde no doubt still fills the northern roads." A breeze was drawing most of the smoke away from the cave mouth so sleeping inside should not be too bad that night.

"Perhaps."

Keff added dried spices to the bubbling contents of the stew pot. "Or maybe they're all at the city by now."

"I doubt that we could be so lucky."

"We were lucky enough to catch that rabbit."

Mica smiled. "I didn't know if I still had the skills to bring one down with a thrown knife."

"Your knife-throwing skills are matched solely by your animal-skinning skills." Janos smiled. "Somehow the skinning of small woodland animals never came up in the labouratorium."

"A most regrettable lack of skill. I shall have to teach you all such talents as we journey." Mica matched Janos's grin with one of his own. "I would hate to see a scholar lacking such a basic talent."

"We have fled the city as we planned...but now what?"

"So now we must settle upon a course of action. Where do we go?"

"If we flee west, we might be able to reach the Transcendent Bridge."

"And establish ourselves in Mirtoxas?"

"No doubt their court will welcome learned scholars."

"No doubt. Or else we might be executed as wizards."

"I don't recall the Thorns being overly enthusiastic about worshipping the One God."

"They were supporters of all religions. Gabrielle was raised in the old ways, I think." Mica frowned, trying to recall vague memories of gossip overheard at Court. "Imperial decrees have little force that far from the capitol. And much less still with each garrison withdrawn to the north."

"West is a possibility."

"I still prefer to head east."

"Across the Bay?" Janos looked at her.

"Yes," Sapphire said. "The lands there are almost certainly free of the Horde. Can you say the same about the road west to Mirtoxas?"

"No," Mica admitted.

"So we head north?" Keff asked. "Through the Gap of Tears and then around the edge of the Wastelands? Or do we skirt the Krindle Mountains and follow the coast around the Bay?"

"We could head south into Ceres. Maybe take the Golden Road." So named for the amount of grain that Ceres shipped to the capitol and other northern towns. "On the other hand, maybe we should avoid the main roads and stick to lesser ones. We would be less likely to encounter patrols along such paths." Whether Imperial or Keli'cairn, neither would be safe to meet. "We should be able to find a ship to ferry us across the mouth of the Bay."

"That might be costly. I doubt there are many ships still there. Half the ships of the known world are sailing the Bay right now, ferrying refugees from the capitol."

"My Lady, what are you thoughts?"

"We shall see." She yawned. "I suggest that we sleep on these matters."

* * *

The cave was fairly bright when Janos opened his eyes and looked around.

His companions sat by the cavern mouth, quiet and still.

A rumbling echoed and Janos wondered if it heralded an approaching storm. "Is that thunder?" he asked as the sound continued far longer than any thunderbolt should.

"'Tis the Horde passing us by." Mica was resting his right hand on his sword hilt, though he had not yet drawn the blade from its sheath. "That is the sound of men marching and horses' hooves and wagon wheels in their uncounted hundreds. I woke to the sound at dawn."

"And we awoke to hear it, so here we hide." Keff grinned weakly. "I wondered how you could sleep through that."

"I did wonder why you let me oversleep." Janos glanced up at the sun. "Since dawn you say?" Judging the sun's position made him shiver. "But that was hours ago!"

"The Horde is huge." Mica sounded calm. "The tribes travel across the land in numbers uncounted."

"Ye *Gods*."

"No hot tea this morning." Keff gestured to the stack of cold firewood. "No fire at all." He still wore his cloak.

"We don't want them to see the smoke," Mica explained. "It would be ironic if we escaped the city only be captured just outside the walls."

"I did not know the Horde was so near." Janos felt his legs getting weak so he hastily sat down in the dirt. "Ye Gods! Scarcely a day's ride from the city walls."

"None of us knew that."

"The Horde ride fast, Sapphire. Faster than most would credit them."

* * *

"Is the mule still there?"

"Aye. Grazing contentedly." Mica shrugged. "I tethered him in the pasture there with plenty of rope. He can wander and eat without our supervision."

"What if he makes a noise?"

"Mules would rather eat than bray," Mica said. "Assuming no one shoots him with a stray arrow, why should he make any sound?"

"But what if—"

"They won't hear it over their own noise." Janos doubted anything would be heard over the rumble of the Horde on the move.

"They're still marching?"

"Aye."

Janos peered out of the cavern mouth. He saw nothing through the screen of pine trees and shrubs. "It sounds so close."

"Sound travels well in this valley." Sapphire tilted her head slightly to the left. "They could be passing by a league or two from here...or they could be just beyond those pines."

What if the mule does *make a sound?* Janos shivered. "And we're just sitting here?"

"Do you have a better idea?"

"No. Hiding is fine with me." Janos looked around for one of the wineskins. *Don't let us have left it on the mule's packs.*

Mica tossed it to him. "Go easily with it. We shall need our wits around us if we are discovered."

"I know." In truth, Janos wanted nothing more than to drown his fears in the wine.

"If we wanted, we could creep out and spy a glimpse of the Horde."

"No!" Janos exclaimed as Keff half-rose. "That is, I would prefer not too. Let them remain a faceless mystery. A terror without shape. 'Gaze not upon the basilisk.' I am staying here."

"Suit yourself."

"Keff, you're staying too."

"But—"

"Sit down," Sapphire warned, "or I will have Mica tie you like a goose."

Keff grumbled, but he sat back down and chewed at his lip.

Night fell and still the rumble of horses growled from beyond the trees.

"All day marching and still no end to them?" Keff munched his bread and hard cheese. "Still, it now sounds like they're pitching camp."

"The Horde is far larger than I feared."

"And I, Janos." Mica was staring off towards the unseen capitol with haunted eyes. "I should be back there."

"Even united, I do not think the city could have been held." Sapphire placed her hand on his arm. "What good could one more sword do back there?" she asked. "One more warrior?"

"It was place," he said simply. "My oath."

"You fulfilled your oath. Gods, Mica, you served with loyalty even after the nobles whom you swore to obey tore the Court asunder. If you had stayed, you would only have died there." Janos shook his head.

"My place was there."

"Not against such odds, Mica. Not against such hatred."

"I don't hate the Horde."

"Nor did most of us hate them."

"The war has come and we are faced with violence that we cannot allow to consume us," Sapphire reminded them. "We do not hate the Horde, nor do they hate us. Not as individuals." She paused. "The city, however, hates itself. Pureblood. Half-breed. Elf and Human. The tangles skeins have torn the empire apart."

"I swore an oath to defend the empire until my death."

"Life is so much better than death," Sapphire told him. "The empire is dead...let the living continue breathing."

Mica lowered his head.

"Anyway," Keff pointed out, "on this journey, you're our protector."

Mica lifted his head in surprise. "Surrounded by the enemy, venturing into the empty lands, and I am the best warrior you could find?"

"Yes. Shame about our luck." Janos grinned. "Better than nothing I guess."

Mica snorted. "If we find ourselves accosted, you will see how dearly I could sell my life."

Sapphire took a drink from the wineskin. "I hope that we do not find that need."

* * *

The sun was hiding behind a cloud when the travelers crested a low hill.

"We should have brought the mule wagon."

Janos agreed with his companion's soft grumbling even though he knew they would never have gotten any wagon through those tunnels. The packs were heavy, even with the mule carrying the bulk of their supplies. "And to think that we only brought necessities."

"And our key supplies for our work." Keff adjusted his pack. "I never dreamed that scrolls could be so heavy."

"Try hefting these models." Even while walking with the largest pack on his back, Mica kept one hand on the sword belted at his waist. Back at the labouratorium, he had divided food and water between all of them, though each had then further laden their packs with such things as each deemed essential. *Trust the scholars to take their scrolls and models.* He had attempted to limit himself to additional food and supplies, though Keff had prevailed upon him to carry a few models.

Sapphire seemed amused by the exertion required to carry her own pack. "Maybe we can obtain another mule or a wagon in the next village." She was carrying medicines and personal items she had not yet identified to the others. "Perhaps we can find a mule wagon to buy...or steal."

"If we can find one. We've been walking for days."

"And we'll walk further still, Keff." Ten days since they had left the cave—after hiding there for three full days while the Horde passed by them. "We'll walk until our legs give out."

"This area is not pure wilderness. There must be villages or at least farms."

"Not many. The main roads into Ceres all lie farther to the west. Which we are avoiding for obvious reasons."

"Not wanting to go to Ceres itself being chief among them."

"And not wanting to encounter Keli'cairn scouts or patrols." Sapphire had a map in her pack. "Otherwise, most traffic went by boat through the Bay. This is one of the lesser roads, seldom used before the invasion I should think."

"Surely Ceres will be sending out patrols?"

"Why should they bother?" Mica countered. "The local governors know perfectly well where the Horde is coming from and they know what strength their garrisons still stand at." He shook his head. "The Emperor pulled almost every soldier back to the capitol in the last few moons. With its fall, there is nothing left to oppose the Horde. At least not this side of the Whitewater," he amended.

"So assuming the city withstands the siege for any length of time," and Janos truly doubted that it would have held for more than a day or two, "the Horde will be moving farther south." He listened constantly for sounds of horsemen.

"Not for some time," Mica countered. "They will be looting the city for days...and they will see little need to press on after such a victory. We have some time before any of the Horde continues south."

"We'll never reach the mouth of the Bay before they overtake us!"

"We don't need to reach the mouth."

"But the port is there."

"There should be villages long before that." Sapphire smiled. "Trust me in this."

"Of course we trust you, my Lady." Janos paused. "You led us safely from the city. We cannot fault your confidence now."

"I am glad to hear that." She raised her arm to point. "Because there is a village. Lisbet's Respite I believe is the name. It is small, but we should be able to relax for a day or two."

"Wow, she's good." Keff was grinning. "A proper bed tonight."

"A bath," Janos sighed.

"Hot food." Mica started walking again.

Chapter Fourteen

The village was small with only a handful of businesses and shops. "Little more than a wide spot in the road," was how Keff described it.

"What more do you need?" Mica asked him. "It has all of the essentials." He pointed to each in turn. "A blacksmith shop. An inn. A butcher. And a few houses to support them and their families."

"Hardly enough homes to support a business."

"Aye, but what of the farms? No doubt there are many scattered about here."

"Plus there is traffic along the road." Sapphire walked towards the inn. "Or at least there was before the invasion. I believe Lisbet's Respite is about three day's horse ride from Salidaralesom."

"I am willing to agree to that." Mica considered in his head. "Yes, that would be about right. A good place for a village to stand."

Sapphire nodded. "There are several such between here and the mouth ports. Once there was a village spaced out in such a way that you could shelter each night. Most of them are gone now. Lost to wars and rebellions and a lack of traffic along this road."

"You are a veritable font of knowledge, my Lady."

"I had knowledgeable teachers as a child."

* * *

The innkeeper stared at the party as they stepped through his door. The handful of patrons paused in their drinking to stare as well.

"Good evening, my Lady. Welcome to the Wanderer's Respite." The innkeeper approached with a cautious bow. Sapphire was dressed in a gown of the richest cloth, so it was only natural that he should address her. "Kurt Webber, at your ladyship's service." He eyed Mica nervously. The man's armour and sword marked him as her guard at the least, possibly even a Guardsman of the city.

"I am Sapphire, of House Barrelweight." Sapphire pulled coins from her belt pouch. "Rooms for the night and a good meal if you please. We might be traveling on in the morning, but I am not sure yet. I might desire to rest for a few days. Our journey has been arduous and we have many leagues yet to travel."

"Of course, my Lady. Good rooms we have here. The best for leagues."

"You have the *only* rooms for leagues," Keff murmured.

Janos nudged him. "Hush."

"We have a mule hitched outside."

"Chas, see to stabling the lady's mule." A scrawny youth stopped polishing a table and hurried out the door. "I have a fine room for you, my Lady. And one right next door for your guard." He nodded to Mica. "I fear your..." he looked askance at Janos and Keff, "servants will be settled on the lower floor."

"That is acceptable." She nodded to him.

"*Servants?*"

Janos nudged Keff again.

"I would enjoy a hot bath," Sapphire announced. "We have been traveling for many days."

"Fleeing the city," one of the other patrons said. "Meaning no offence," he added hastily.

"None taken."

"We haven't had visitors here in almost a year." The innkeeper sighed. "I fear that the Emperor, may he rule forever, has forgotten about us."

"No Emperor, no taxman." The man's companions looked horrified at his attempted jest.

"We're not tax collectors," Janos reassured them. "Merely humble scholars."

"I see."

"Baths first, then we shall consider dinner."

"There's stew in the kitchen. And the baths are around at the back. I fear there's only one tub."

"We shall make do." Sapphire gestured for the innkeeper to lead her to her room. "Lead us, good Sir."

* * *

The common room was crowded. It seemed that every person in the village, and many of the surrounding farms, had crowded together to see the travelers.

Bathed and dressed in clean clothes, Janos felt like being part of a crowd. *They would not have appreciated our presence before the baths. Even if he had been required to share the wooden tub with Keff. I wonder how Mica enjoyed his bath with Sapphire?* Though neither had spoken of it, he had little doubt that the two *had* shared their bath water. The others were already present.

"The wine is passable, the ale better." Mica was looking quite cheerful as he poured another mug.

"I'll take wine. Ale bothers my stomach."

"The stew will fill your stomach better than wine." Keff was scrapping the bottom of his bowl. "'Tis good."

Janos accepted a bowl and a loaf of crusty bread. *It smells wonderful.*

Conversation flowed, the locals offering advice on weather and the road, while the travelers shared what they knew of news and rumours from around the Empire.

Every topic kept returning to the same subject.

"The Horde will be coming this way, sooner or later."

"That we know all too well. The lack of traffic along the road...."

"Won't stop the Horde from coming. Once they have taken the City, they'll set about securing the rest of the countryside. They will likely focus on the Golden Road into Ceres, but I'm sure they'll come down the other roads as well."

"It will just likely take them a bit longer."

"The Horde will cover the land."

"Aye, all the way to the Sea."

A farmer's wife sighed loudly. "Is there no hope that the capitol still stands?" she asked.

"None that I can see," Mica told the woman bluntly.

"But his Majesty—"

"Was rumoured to be dead even before we left the City."

Janos nodded. "We left a city collapsing in upon itself. A city consumed by riot and fire. The Court was fighting itself, the Guards were confused, and there was pitched battle in the streets. Once the Horde reached the walls, I do not see how the factions could have pulled together fast enough to stop them."

The mood turned glum.

"Does anyone have a mule for sale?" Keff asked as he scraped his bowl clean with a chunk of bread. "We could use another one. A cart would be nice too."

"Old Thom might sell you his mule," one farmer suggested. "He doesn't use it much anymore. Don't know anyone with a wagon to sell though."

"Anyone smart will keep their wagon and use it to flee." The speaker was a particularly plump woman. "Before the Horde descend upon us and rape us in our beds."

"Small fear you should have of *that*," the innkeeper muttered just loud enough for Janos to hear. "Not unless they have some perverse love of goats."

Janos tried not to laugh aloud. *She does look rather goatish.*

"Where can we run?" someone asked. "The Horde have taken the northlands and are moving south faster than we could run."

"We could flee west...try to reach Mirtoxas."

"You could sail into the Sea of Storms and see what lays to the south. If the pirates and Sea-Elves don't sink you first."

"So we just stay here?"

"Aye." The old man puffed on his pipe. "We are farmers and herders. The Horde will need our services to grow their food. The Empire is dead and gone...so now we just labour for new masters."

"Higher taxes."

"Better higher taxes than dead in your bed."

* * *

"My Lady?" Janos blinked.

"It is I."

"Your hair!"

"With the city behind us, I felt it was time for a change." She held up a lock of her now silvery-blonde hair. "What do you think?"

"It is...different."

"I like it." Mica smiled at her. "Much better than the red. Golden tresses suit you very well."

"Another of my brother's foolish restrictions. Dying my hair in some foul potion every moon-quarter. Anything to further obscure the truth of our bloodline." She paused. "Those days are past. I am of Elf-Blood and I am proud of it."

"And your eyes?" Keff said. "They didn't used to be that tilted."

"A little make-up can conceal or obscure many things. I was highly practiced in said arts, living with my brother." She shook out her hair. "I am glad to be done with such disguises."

* * *

"So now that we have left the village behind, do we still ride south?"

"I was thinking of a different path," Sapphire said.

"I wondered why we had left the main road to follow this cow path." The trees grew close and the undergrowth had all but obscured the path Sapphire was leading them along.

"There should be a boat hidden nearby. A private cove my family knew of." Sapphire gestured to the south. "We shall head that way."

"Aye, my Lady. We will accept your apparently superior knowledge of the area."

Mica smiled. "Now I see why you knew so much about the *Respite* and the condition of the road."

"I haven't traveled this way since I was a girl." Sapphire had a new-found spring in her step.

"Did your brother travel with you?"

"My brother had no wish to learn. He preferred to forget about the past. His loss."

"Indeed."

Chapter Fifteen

The thick forest growth gave way to open clearing with surprising suddenness.

"We have arrived."

"We have? Arrived where?"

"Some property that once belonged to my mother's mother and back through the long generations. I am not certain just how long we maintained a house on these lands." Sapphire gestured at the Bay. "It has a fine view, does it not?" She walked along the edge of a garden, long since reclaimed by the wild.

"The house needs a little work." Keff kept his voice light.

The manor house was a crumbling ruin now. Once it had no doubt been glorious, from what traces could still be seen of it. A central block with two flanking towers, built of gray limestone. Most of the roof had long-since fallen in, and the rightmost tower was now little more than a mound of stone.

"My grandmother used to bring me here when I was a child." Sapphire's voice held the warmth of a fond memory. "We would spend long summer days lounging by the water's edge. She taught me the names of all the birds and how to call them into my hand. She taught me of herbs and potions and poultices."

"She was a wise woman."

"She was indeed."

"I never knew my family," Keff mused. "They died after being sold on the slavers' block."

Janos grimaced.

"She is buried here, overlooking the river." Sapphire stopped by a small pile of rocks. "I miss her." She bowed her head a moment in quiet prayer.

"Did you spend time with your mother here?"

"My mother was much like my brother." Sapphire's voice held little warmth now. "She despised her Elf-Blood and refused to acknowledge the heritage granny had tried to teach us. She let the house fall into disrepair and never came here."

Keff tethered the mule to a branch, leaving him enough rope that he could wander a bit and graze on the overgrown lawn.

"We shall make our camp here tonight."

"We will?"

"It makes the most sense, does it not?" Sapphire approached the closed door. "We can rest in safety. And out of the rain." She glanced up at the cloudy sky. "It will rain tonight." She reached for the handle. "Granny never locked her door."

"Trusting woman," Mica murmured over the creaking of rusted hinges.

* * *

The house interior still bore traces of its former glory and elegance. Tapestries hung on the walls, their once-vibrant colours now faded, the cloth weather-tattered and moth-eaten.

"The stairs look unsafe."

"So we'll stay out of the tower." Mica looked around, his dark eyes quickly taking stock of everything in the room and scanning for potential threats.

"There is no danger here."

"I won't need my armour tonight then." He rested his hand on his sword. "There is not much left here."

"Neither my mother nor my brother approved of our Elf-Blood, but they were practical enough to strip the house of whatever they thought they could sell." Sapphire pushed open a door. "Even the library is empty." The rows of shelves looked so barren.

"We can sleep here. We should get some shelter from the night." There were clouds darkening the sky and she expected rain before dusk fell. "I think there are candles still."

"I see one." Keff picked up the wooden candelabra from a wall shelf. "This is beautiful carving."

"Elf work," Janos told him. "Even the most practical of items should still be made beautiful. 'Tis such craftsmanship you seldom see these days."

"I'd like to see the kitchen. Maybe we can find something worth eating."

The kitchen was as empty as the rest of the house. A few oddments had been left behind, but mostly anything portable or valuable had been carried off.

"No food."

"There might be something still growing wild in the gardens."

"I'll go and look."

"Mica, go with him. Gather whatever you can find. We'll have provisions for our journey."

"As you wish." Mica picked some empty sacks from a corner. "These will suffice I trust. Coming, Keff?"

Keff was eyeing a stairwell. "I was thinking about going down there," he said.

"Into the cellar?"

"Sure, I wanted to go and see what's down there."

"Some empty storerooms most likely. If the upstairs is this empty, then I am certain my dear family would have stripped the storerooms too."

"Well, I can still look, can't I?"

"Let him," Janos said. "What harm is there?"

"I'll go with him," Mica announced.

Janos watched them descend the stairs.

"What is your opinion of all this?"

Janos turned and looked at her. "I think that we are in some danger here," he admitted, "though less that I would expect."

"There is no danger here."

"The Horde may yet follow us...this house cannot become a sanctuary for long."

"You are the ever-practical one." Sapphire nodded. "I know that we cannot remain for long. Our journey is set and we will venture across the Bay in due time. A few days' rest will not harm us now. The road was more difficult than I had expected."

"You have not complained."

"What use would there have been in my complaining?" she asked him. "We could not remain in the city. We had to leave. We had to take the road." She shrugged again. "The journeys of my youth were less taxing."

"And mine. I do enjoy long journeys. I am content within a city." He laughed bitterly. "Some Elf...content with city life."

"There are many Elf-kin, Janos. Your blood no more disposes you to enjoy forest camps than Keff's blood will make a miner of him."

"Success!" Keff emerged from the basement with a dusty Mica in tow. "Wine!"

"Wine?" Sapphire looked surprised. "I would not have expected there to be wine in the cellar."

"I was looking in the storeroom and I found three bottles. Lots of empty crates and barrels. A few broken bottles and smashed pottery. Couple of dead mice too. And these bottles pushed way into a dark shadowy corner."

"Did your granny have good taste?"

"Not that I know of. I was just a child then and did not drink wine."

"We'll try it later." Mica took the bottles from Keff's hands and set them onto the counter. "Come on." He handed Keff the sacks. "We have plants to harvest."

Chapter Sixteen

The gardens were overgrown. The plants grew lush and rampant.

"The apples were always good." Sapphire plucked a ripe one from a low branch and bit into it. "Yes, 'tis very sweet."

Janos eyed the trees. "She had a fair-sized orchard."

"Aye, she did. It was larger once, but many of the trees were cut down when I was younger."

"I'm surprised your mother didn't sell the property if she tried to sell everything else."

"She did."

"Oh."

"But no one wanted it. A handful of people came out to look at it, but they left claiming that ghosts had chased them away." The lady laughed lightly. "Such tales they told."

"I see." Janos frowned. "True ghosts...or a bit of child's play?"

"A bit of both perhaps."

Mica glanced at them, and then returned to his harvesting.

"So the property fell into disuse and disrepair. I don't think my brother even remembered it existed." A smile played at her lips. "So it became mine by default."

Keff picked up a half-filled sack of roots. "Too far from the capitol for most people to want to bother with it I'd think."

"That was a common fault, yes. But it made a nice summer home. Away from the heat and boredom of the city." Sapphire paused. "I should check the herb gardens before we leave. There might some useful plants growing there."

"And do we still plan to cross the Bay by your boat?"

"Unless you know how to fly, friend Janos." Sapphire grinned as she stepped lightly along an overgrown pathway. "I would be willing enough to try flying if you have learned the secrets of the birds?"

"No, not yet." Janos shook his head. *Men fly like birds? 'Tis not likely.*

"Then we take the boat. It's tied up down here by the dock."

The dock extended a short way into the water and a boat was tethered to it.

"Is that what you sought, my Lady?" Janos eyed the small boat with some apprehension.

"It is just as I remember it."

The boat was small and roughly-built. The timbers were weathered and gray, though the seams were still caulked tight.

"It's not pretty."

"No, but it is quite safe. I have sailed in it many times." Sapphire stepped from the shore onto the deck. "There should be a sail, yes right here."

"Do you know how to sail it?" Janos asked.

"I sailed with my grandmother many times as a child. I'm certain we can figure it out." She smiled. "The blood of Sea-Elves flows within my veins. Surely it cannot be too difficult."

Mica frowned, but stepped into the boat and helped lift the sail. "You two are scholars, eh? Let's see a demonstration of your vaunted brainpower."

Janos sighed. "Is the mule going to ride with us?"

"I see no reason why it should not. Cut some reeds for him to stand on and eat and he will be fine."

"I'll see what I can find." Janos took his dagger and squelched along the muddy bank towards the bulrushes.

Keff and Mica had managed to get the sail attached to the rigging.

Sapphire nodded approvingly. "The breeze should push us across the Bay."

"It had better. I'm not rowing."

Keff laughed. "I'm not swimming across."

Janos tossed another arm-load of cut reeds into the bow. "That should be enough."

"Then we can cast-off at dawn."

* * *

Sapphire tossed herbs into the pot and gave it stir.

"Smells good."

"A soldiers always thinks about food."

Mica grinned. "Due to a lack of good food being delivered."

"The chance to eat well is not one to be passed by," Keff added. "There has been little enough chance of such while on this flight."

"We can scarcely sit around and cook stew with the Horde so close."

"Tomorrow we must move."

"Sapphire?"

"Janos and I spoke earlier. This house cannot be a refuge for long."

"Sadly, no."

"We have food and herbs."

"We have a place to rest."

"We're dry." Rain was splashing against the windows. "It's going to be wet for a few days."

"How do you know?"

Sapphire smiled. "A feeling."

"Then we rest here until the storm passes." Mica filled a bowl with hot stew. "Mmm."

"So we are set then? We sail the Bay?"

"Aye."

Janos sighed. "So be it."

"'Tis a beautiful day."

"It should be after three days of rain."

"Is the boat still dry?"

"Of course."

Janos eyed the water and the boat with some trepidation.

Sapphire had placed their packs in the boat. "Help me with this." She gestured towards two thick planks. "We'll make a bridge for the mule."

Once the boards were laid from the deck to the shore, it took only a little effort to convince the mule to board the boat.

Keff untied the ropes.

"Maybe we'll see a nymph or two."

"That would be useful," Sapphire agreed.

"That would be dangerous!" Janos protested.

The wind gusted and filled the sails.

Chapter Seventeen

The Bay of Torenth was quiet as they sailed it. A strong breeze filled the sails and the boat made good time. Sapphire held the tiller in a careful grip. "We should reach the far shore by morning if this wind holds."

"And if it doesn't?"

"Then we ride wherever the waves will carry us."

"You seem unworried by that prospect, my Lady."

"I cannot control the winds or the waves, Janos." She waved her hand idly and her ruby ring glinted. "If the Gods wish to blow us clear back to Salidaralesom, then that is where we will end up."

"I hope not."

"We might end up blowing out into the Sea of Storms."

"Gods, I hope to be spared that fate as well."

"You don't like sailing, do you?"

Janos looked at Mica. "No, I most certainly do not." He felt his stomach lurch in sympathy with the boat as it rode the waves. "I begin to think that walking through the Horde and around the top of the Bay was not such a bad idea after all."

Sapphire laughed.

"Even the mule isn't complaining half as much as you," Mica pointed out dryly.

"He is content with his reeds and grain."

"So maybe we should tie a sack to your face and just let you eat in peace." The others echoed Keff's hearty laughter.

Janos sighed.

The boat sailed towards the shore.

"At last." Janos sighed with relief. "Gods, if I should reach the shore alive I vow never to set foot on a boat again."

"The crossing wasn't so bad," Mica told him. "No storms. No pirates."

"No sea dragons," Keff added.

"I have never heard of any sea dragons in the Bay of Torenth." Sapphire shook her head at such an absurd thought.

"I see ruins."

At Mica's startled outburst, Janos forgot about his stomach. "Let me see." He took the far-seer tube from Mica and held it to his eye. "Where?"

"Straight ahead of you."

Janos squinted at the rocky cliffs. "We would be reaching shore at dusk," he grumbled while looking again. "You're right. I do see ruins ahead. It looks like a city."

"A city?" Keff reached for the tube. "But what city is over here?"

"Not one that I am familiar with," Sapphire said. She was still holding the rudder. "But I think we are going to be landing near it." The current was strong, even as the wind faltered.

The boat beached on the rocky shore.

A few hundred paces from the water's edge, the remains of a wall stood. Only a few stretches of stone were still piled taller than a man, as most of the former wall was now little more than mounds of weed-covered rubble.

Mica and Keff pulled the boat into place on the beach.

"Is it safe?" Janos asked.

"'Tis deserted." Mica gestured with his arm. "I see no candles nor fires glowing. I smell no smoke. And I hear nothing save the waves and the night birds."

"Mica is correct. I think that the city is deserted. Apparently it has been for some time." Sapphire had lit a torch. "Shall we explore?"

"I don't know that it is safe. I said it appeared deserted." Mica had his sword drawn and held it ready. "Just because there are no candles or fires, there could still be dangers."

"I think not."

"Bandits could be hiding inside. Animals, my Lady, could be nesting there."

"Or falling rubble. If the city has been abandoned, then the buildings will be in a state of disrepair. Exploration would be far safer by daylight."

Sapphire nodded with obvious reluctance. "Then I suggest that we explore just enough to find a chamber where we might camp for the night."

"Agreed." Mica led the way, still holding his sword as if he expected to be attacked by every shadow.

* * *

A small building just inside the crumbling wall was mostly intact. Janos and Keff started a small fire with driftwood gathered from the beach while Sapphire curried the mule and tethered the beast in a second room. Mica left them alone while he made a quick patrol of the surrounded ruins.

At length he returned, dusty but unharmed. "No sign of anything larger than a bat," he reported. "The buildings are abandoned but still mostly intact. Whomever built this city was skilled."

"I have my suspicions."

Janos looked at the lady. "You think this is one of the Elf cities?"

"Aye." She poured a small mug of wine from their stores. "The natural harbour here would have appealed to them, methinks."

"Then maybe we will find treasure."

"I suspect that the Elves took their treasure when they left this city."

Keff looked disappointed. He ran his hand through his red hair. "All of it?"

"Probably."

"But we will learn more tomorrow. I suggest that we get a good night's sleep now and spend the daylight exploring some of the ruins. Maybe we can find something of use for us."

"A wise plan. I shall take the first watch," Mica announced. "In case anything is lurking out there and getting bold."

"And if something *is* lurking," Keff asked, "and it gets bold later?"

"I'm a very fast waker," Mica told him with a feral grin.

* * *

Janos sighed. "I hate night watch." Hours of restlessness wrapped in his cloak while his companions slumbered in their cloaks.

The wind murmured through the ruins and the mule blinked sleepily as the Half-Elf walked past.

Janos sighed. "This is going to be a long night."

Chapter Eighteen

"The moon is bright."

"The Gods see fit to illuminate our path."

"The road is empty. I hope the forest is equally empty." Janos eyed the trees and grimaced. "I have never cared overmuch for wild places."

"You could have stayed back in the capitol." Keff snickered.

"No, thank you."

"We're quite safe." The Horde is on the far side of the Bay. There should be no settlements anywhere nearby for days and days."

"That makes me feel so much better."

"I wish we could have explored the ruins more. I'm sure we would have found something of worth back there."

"We saw only ruins, Keff. Dust and stone. There was nothing left to take."

"The survivors of the old Kingdoms have fled the easily reached lands. They have gone far beyond the Human borders." Sapphire smiled. "They will have rebuilt their cities there."

"You seem so certain?"

She smiled at them. "I have heard stories."

One particularly twisted tree loomed on their right, reaching its branches towards the path.

"That is one ugly tree," Keff commented.

An angry buzz filled the air.

"What's that?"

"Hellwasps!" Sapphire swore.

"Great."

Hundreds of blood-red wasps billowed out of the tree. They were thumb-sized, with iridescent green compound eyes.

"What do we do?"

"Run!" Sapphire shook her head. "You can't fight them with your sword, Mica."

They ran, tugging at the mule.

The swarm loomed behind them.

Sapphire murmured something under her breath.

"Magic?"

"A little wind." The breeze gusted. "With luck it will blow them away."

"You hope."

"Yes, I do."

They collapsed to the ground, panting and gasping for breath. "I think we have outrun the swarm."

"Gods, I hope so. I cannot run another step."

"A clever trick with the breeze, my Lady." Mica fanned his face.

"A simple thing." Sapphire reached for a water bottle. "Magic flows easily here...something to do with the wildness of nature I believe."

"So now what?"

"We continue to march southward."

"South?"

"Yes, south. Toward the Sea of Storms."

"We're not going to sail the Sea?"

"No, Janos, we're not."

"Thank the Gods."

"We walk...once we regain our breath."

Chapter Nineteen

The Sea of Storms lay beyond the cove, stretching into the distance. Janos lifted a far-seer tube to his eyes and looked out. "I only see a few gulls." The view was almost hypnotic, but he pulled his gaze along the shoreline. Waves lapped against the white sandy beach.

And there was the city.

He gasped and almost dropped the tube.

The citadel crested the top of a hill. A wall of white stone surrounded the city, even along the water, with spaced towers rising thrice the wall's height. The stone of both towers and wall were flecked with silver that shone in the sunlight. More towers rose from within the city's heart.

"'Tis a wonder!" Janos breathed.

"The true heart of our former glory," Sapphire told her party. "It has been too long since I last looked upon the Shining Walls of Solace." She grinned. "Actually, this is the first time I have seen the Shining Walls for real."

"For real?"

"Scrye stones only show so much," she replied.

"But I thought the Empire destroyed your capitol?"

"That was the newer capital and it belonged more to the Plain-Elves. The Sea-Elves did not bother too much with it. This is Castille Alabaster. One is the oldest of our cities still standing. 'Tis likely the oldest city in the world." She spurred her horse forward. "Come, let us ride."

The gates were closed. Polished silver, carved with runes and flowers.

"No guards?" Mica asked. "How trusting." He didn't even see guards patrolling the battlements. "An enemy could overrun you before you even knew they were coming!"

"We are quite safe. The city has many defences placed upon it. Our wards shelter us from the ill-intentions of outsiders."

"Do we knock?" Janos asked.

Sapphire held up her hand. "I wish to enter!" Her ring sparkled with a rich inner flame.

The gates swung open without a sound.

"Magic."

"A simple trick, Mica."

"A good one nonetheless."

The streets of Solace were carpeted in lush moss. Trees grew lush and many were laden with fruit. Flowers blossomed in profusion, filling the air with a multitude of scents. Birds sang melodies from the trees.

"A garden on every corner," Keff murmured.

"'Tis like the paradise promised by the One God."

"We live in harmony with nature. This is our world."

"I feel out of place."

"Do not fear, Mica. You will be made welcome here." Sapphire smiled. "All are welcome here...save those who bring evil and corruption in their hearts."

"Safety...not a prize to be overlooked in these times."

Elves approached from within the city. They wore tunics and tight breeches of brightly coloured cloth. The fabrics were light and airy.

Sapphire smiled warmly at a group. "Elder."

"Sapphire, you have returned to us." He made an elaborate gesture with his hands. "Welcome!"

"You know him?"

"Oh yes," she agreed. "He visited my grandmother's house."

"A fine woman. We were sorrowed to hear of her passing."

The Elves studied the travelers.

"You have traveled far it seems."

"We have fled from the capitol."

"Ahead of the Horde."

"Aye."

"Mica Feldspar was a captain of the Emperor's Guard. These are Janos and Keff, scholars of some skill and arcane knowledge."

"Your companions are welcome here, Lady Sapphire. Word of the Horde's advance has come to our ears. We hope the Keli'cairn will not venture onto this side of the Bay, but we prepare for whatever actions we must in these dark days." His eyes skimmed across the boys. "He has Elf-blood."

"Yes." Janos nodded.

"'Tis the Luminary!" Elder Sunmantle stared and made a peculiar gesture in the air with his left hand. "The Eye of the All-Father."

"The what?"

"An ancient symbol of our people." The Elf sounded amazed. "No one has borne such an emblem in centuries."

"It seems common enough in your art."

"Its use is all-but-forbidden...only those so chosen may wear it." He looked at the Sapphire. "Ye did not tell him?" he asked suspiciously.

"Nay, Elder, for why should I have done so?"

"Then where did the half-breed come across it?"

"It was given to me."

"By whom?"

"A...woman," he finished lamely. "She met me in a tavern and gave it to me."

"Shouldn't you be the one to give a woman in a tavern a pretty bauble?" Keff asked innocently.

"Shut up!"

"A woman gave you this prize?" the Elder asked.

"Yes."

"Interesting."

Sapphire nodded. "I knew it was a sin for him to wear it, but still my heart hinted that he could be the one foretold."

"Or he could be a tomb-thief," another Elf spoke up.

"We shall have to ponder this matter."

* * *

Janos looked around the park meadow. "So you are not all Elf-kind?"

"We have humans in our midst too." The man was clad in roughly-dressed animal skins. "The Hillmen are our friends."

"Nickel Ironhelm." The man's red beard was immensely bushy, as were his eyebrows. "A pleasure to meet you at last."

"Likewise." Janos frowned. "You've heard of me?"

"Hasn't everyone?" He seemed genuinely surprised by Janos's question. "Stories about your inventions have been coming to us for years now. Lots of interesting things you've been working on. Can't wait to get you jawing with some of our thinking-types."

"I had no idea."

"The Hillmen provide us with ores and jewels. We give them food and medicines."

"Both treasures very hard to come by underground."

"And there are some mostly-human settlements further east. We have some trade arrangements with them, initiated at their inclination and subject to their desire for contact."

"This land sounds idyllic."

"We have always sought to live in harmony with nature, following its laws as we must."

"And the Empire?"

"Holds no sway here...nor have its emperors ever visited these shores."

* * *

"I could be happy here." Janos turned to his companions. "I have spent much time within their libraratorium. So much reading there. So much hidden knowledge. Scrolls that date back before the Empire first rose."

"They have a kraken hide in there!"

"I saw it, Keff."

Sapphire smiled warmly. "I am content to be among my people."

"I'm not leaving your side," Mica told her.

"The Hillmen said I can go and study with them. They have secrets of smith craft and mining that we've never imagined. I'm going to write a treatise on them." Keff dropped a handwritten scroll onto the ground. "I think we've found our new home."

"Yes." Janos felt a giddy sense of relief within him. "Home at last."

Part Three: Conflagration

Chapter Twenty

Janos stepped carefully around the sprawling rose-of-the-sun. Though many enjoyed the scent of the large yellow blossoms, he cared little for the thorns that covered most the viney growth. *Too many times pricking myself upon those cursed things.*

Two yellow-haired children scurried past him. "Good morning, Uncle!" they called out.

"Good morning Thorn, Marigold." He could only smile as the two youngsters vanished at a run. "So busy at that age...so full of energy." He was still smiling when he rounded the corner of the arboretum and found Mica and Sapphire seated there, sharing their morning tea.

Birds chirped loudly at him.

"Here for the council?" Sapphire asked him. "Or for the tea?"

"The tea now, council later." Janos took the cup and settled himself onto the ground. "I had never expected to get used to sitting on moss," he told them as he gave his tunic a tug into place, "but after so many years, I think that I would be unused to chairs."

"You have a chair in your athenaeum." Mica smiled indulgently at his friend. "You had it carved especially."

Janos nodded. "I have a few chairs true...but the moss is surprisingly comfortable. Even my knees have stopped aching."

"Ten years." Sapphire sipped her tea with a serene and mysterious smile on her lips.

"They've passed in an eye-blink." Mica smiled back at her. "But I would consider an eternity too short a time to spend with you." His clothes were still loose on his athletic form.

Sapphire rested her hand on his leg. "And I with you, love."

A figure approached. His green robes swayed as he walked. "Ten years is too short a time to truly savour what we have here."

"How bad is the news, Saturna?" Janos asked.

"The council will be meeting later this day to discuss events." The Elf frowned back at him. "Things are not good."

The splashing of the small waterfall was a soothing backdrop to the chatter from knots of Elves and men. Sunlight glinted off water in both the pond and stream.

"...and I thought it would be months more before I returned to the city here," Keff was saying.

"It's good to see you back." Mica slapped his shoulder. "Very good."

"Is it good to see me as well?" a breathy feminine voice asked.

"What are you doing here?" Janos asked in surprise as he turned to face the speaker.

Amber smiled at him. "The trade in Salidaralesom has dried up of late." She looked radiant, a red dress setting off the gold-like colour of her hair. A necklace hung from her neck and rings adorned her fingers. "I decided it was long past time to come home."

"May the Light Bearers illuminate our path through this troubled time," Elder Sunmantle intoned, his voice cutting through lingering chatter. "Let this Council commence." He paused while everyone took seats upon the moss. The chatter slowly died away. "The Human wars grow ever worse." Elder Sunmantle opened the council with grim tidings. "Despite the totality of the fall of the Salidaran Empire, the Keli'cairn has not been content with their hard-won holdings. The various tribes have fallen into internecine warfare."

"This is good news then." Janos paused as the eyes of the Council shifted to him. "Isn't it?"

A pale grey-skinned reptile skittered past. It had a bullet-shaped head with a large pair of horns above its twitching ears. A similar structure tipped its tail. Mini-lightning crackled along the horns. It looked at Janos and a sharp crack sounded as lighting leapt from its horns.

Janos shook his hand, trying to banish the tingle left by the spark. "Damned pest."

The reptile skittered off.

"It is not good news." Hawkeye represented the scouts. "The tribes fight with little care for what happens to the innocents caught in the middle of the bloodshed. Farms are looted and burned without a care for how the farmers, and their would-be rulers, will live through the winter."

"What of the capitol?"

"Most of the so-called New City was burned when the Keli'cairn Horde sacked it." Amber offered her report in a slightly less breathy voice than she usually used. "The Guardsmen were slaughtered in large numbers, as were any who raised arms against the Horde. It was terrible. Blood in the streets. Fires everywhere. Burning and looting. No safe place for a girl."

"What happened to the Emperor?" Keff asked.

"Dead long before the walls were breached. A handful of nobles were taken captive and sacrificed by the Horde. Most of the Priests of the One God were sacrificed too. A nice show it was."

Janos lowered his head. "I feared it would be so."

"Most of the inner city is still there. The Horde Chieftains divided it amongst themselves. They hold large portions of it, fighting minor battles over territory. The former farmsteads are all but ignored."

"The city is held securely?"

"The walls are still breached and open, many of its towers fallen into rubble. There are few sentries, but the streets teem with tribesmen and women. Entire families are there in their uncounted thousands."

"The Horde always came in huge numbers beyond count," Mica commented softly. "But we never thought of their women or children as being part of those numbers. "Twas always just the men we faced in open battle...always tall warriors in leather armour."

A silence fell on the gathering. Even the birds had fallen silent.

"What about Mirtoxas?"

Hawkeye spoke up: "It stands, Janos. The Transcendent Bridge has been cast down and a line of forts stand endless watch along the Whitewater. Many of those able to flee Salidaralesom fled across the Bridge before it was cast down."

"So what be the problem?" Ironhelm demanded. "If yon tribes fight each other, they threaten us not. Right?"

"The problem is that the Keli'cairn are reunifying. At least certain eastern tribes are uniting under a single banner. The banner that led them to Saliadaralesom." Hawkeye dropped a piece of cloth onto the ground.

"The Red Lightning Bolt." Janos felt a chill.

"The Keli'cairn will march again...in whole or in part. And their scouts are riding eastward."

Janos shook his head. "This land is safe though. The marshes and the mountains will stop the Horde from crossing your borders." They had stopped the Empire for long centuries.

"The Keli'cairn are more persistent than the Imperial Guardsmen ever were."

Mica frowned. "Our scouts and out-riders will do what they can, but our numbers are limited. If even a fraction of the Horde comes..." he voice trailed away.

"We do not believe in maintaining a standing army."

Hawkeye shook his head. "We have the Rangers."

"Lightly armed scouts will be no match for the Horde."

"The real threat will come by sea."

"Pirates?"

"Aye."

"Human pirates, not Sea-Elves such as preyed upon the traders of Salidaralesom."

"Privateers, Janos. The Sea-Elves were defending their rights to the open waters. If your Emperor had been able to have his way, only *his* ships would have sailed upon the seas. Our people were sailing the uncharted waters long before your Imperial Family mastered the art of writing."

Janos smiled. "I concede the point."

Sunmantle made a gesture with his hand. "Mirtoxas has been wise enough to share their harbours with us. We have traded peacefully back and forth for years."

"Even under the Emperor?"

"Under his nose. And those of his tax-collectors."

"And now you just sail right past the lands the Keli'cairn hold."

"We avoid docking at their harbours. It is not overmuch bother for us to avoid docking at such ports as we choose."

"But the Horde aren't sailors." Janos turned his head. "Mica, you told me that the Horde never sailed. They possessed no ships."

"Aye, 'tis true enough. Or it was when I fought them beyond the Gap. They search for passable fords or bridges and cross their troops thusly." He sipped his wine. "Oftentimes that was the only times we could prepare new defences against them. While they searched for fords. I do not think that any of the Horde can swim. They come from the Waterless Wastelands after all."

"And now they come here."

"By ship? How can this be?"

"Do you question the word of my scouts?" Hawkeye demanded. "Or doubt what they saw through your own far-seer tubes?"

"Of course not. I'm just surprised."

"They have no doubt made some bargain with the harbour folk of Meerlasynth. Service in exchange for not being enslaved or slain perhaps." Sunmantle sighed wearily. "The Horde dominates the entire peninsula. They dominate all the lands south of the Waterless Wastelands now."

"At least as far as the Whitewater."

"And now they look towards the east? And over the waves?"

"Their galleons are blocky and slow." Hawkeye sounded scornful. "They will be easy for us to out-sail."

"The Horde have no experience as sailors."

"No, but they are not stupid barbarians either. Their ships are crewed by former Imperials. They have been training and preparing for a decade. If they plan to move now, then they will move in force and we will not be able to stop them."

"Can we stop them?" Mica asked.

"We are Sea-Elves. Masters of all things nautical." Elmwood frowned. "Our xebecs have been sailing the Sea of Storms since before your first emperor was born."

"I do not question your history or skill," Mica soothed, "but I must wonder at how well your fleet will stand against the Horde."

"We will fight, but even if we must sail into range to shoot them with fire arrows."

"And that will make you vulnerable to counter fire from their no doubt superior numbers. So you will need some way to counter their numbers and range."

"Aye. May the Light-Bearers illuminate our path."

"If we cannot stop them at sea, then they will keep coming."

"If they reach our bay and land their troops, then Solace will surely be lost." Sunmantle nodded, his eyes haunted by visions that only he could see. "Fire and sword will ravage the land. Our temples will be defiled. Our treasures will be stolen. Our women will be raped. Our children will be slaughtered. The Dark Times will come upon us again."

"Solace will become *Soulless*."

Sapphire narrowed her eyes. "I will not allow that to happen."

"All of your outriders have yet to return, Hawkeye."

"They will come with news."

"Or the Horde will come."

"I fear that the fate of our land is not yet decided."

"It shall be sooner or later. I will not see our realm conquered by the Keli'cairn." Sunmantle spoke proudly. "We stood against the Empire. We stood while the Plains-Elves fell into shadow."

"Yes, we stood while they died."

"Our secrecy was our best protection. If our armies had marched forth and clashed on the western fields against the Emperor, then we would likely have fallen into defeat as well. Thus, we would now have no army and likely no realm at all."

"Our army is but a shadow of its martial glory."

"Our martial strength is in our ships. We sail the waves with no one to oppose us. That is where our strength rests."

"And by land we sit and wait for the Horde to descend upon and crush us." Janos allowed bitterness to fill his voice. "I sat within the walls of Salidaralesom while the Horde conquered the Empire league by league. I will not sit idly by again while another realm falls."

"Well said."

"So what is thy choice?"

"We will use the thunder-hammers."

Chapter Twenty-One

"Is this fool thing going to work?"

"Ironhelm says that it will."

"Of course it will." The stocky Hillman stood straighter, bringing all his diminutive height to bear. "We be labouring on yon contraptions for weeks."

"Catapults I understand." Mica was examining their workmanship with a careful eye. "But what about the others? Those tubes?"

"The thunder-hammers." Keff smiled. "They're mostly modeled after my own design."

"I see."

"Watch that rock." Ironhelm cranked the wheel and shifted the catapult slightly. "Watch this." He pulled the lever.

The catapult lurched as the armature snapped up and threw a pottery jug. The jug shattered on the ground and exploded with a tremendous roar.

"By all the Gods!" Sunmantle stared at the smoking crater with wide eyes even as the crash still echoed around him. "You have captured the power of the Thundergod!"

"Our thunder dust is noisy but effective." Janos smiled dryly as he looked at the rock still sitting in the field. "We have high hopes for improving the accuracy of the catapults. Eventually."

"And these thunder-hammers?" Sunmantle asked as he studied a bronze tube.

"Show him, Keff."

"The tube, cast from thick and pure bronze, contains a small quantity of thunder dust at the back. We place a stone sphere within the tube like so," he hefted a roughly-hewn sphere into the tube. "And then we light the fuse. Where's my tinder?"

"Use this." Ironhelm handed over his pipe.

"This will be loud," Janos warned as the fuse caught and Keff turned and ran away from the tube.

"Ye dropped my pipe."

"Later!"

The fuse burned down and a roar sounded. Sulfurous smoke belched from the bronze tube and clumps of dirt fountained into the air.

"Ye Gods," Mica swore.

"'Tis a fine weapon you have delivered to us," Hawkeye told the two scholars. "Excellent work."

Sunmantle frowned at the second crater. "I know not if I care for such deliverance," he said grimly. "This seems a power of dark sorcery."

"Nonsense," Keff protested. "'Tis only natural law. Minerals mixed and set alight to create a force that propels the rock spheres in flight."

"Natural law twisted."

"It's our only hope to survive the onslaught of the Keli'cairn."

Sunmantle eyed him grimly. "If you so believe, Hawkeye."

"I do."

"The war comes upon us."

"The same war we fled from. Ten years of peace, now lost." Janos watched a room full of workers grinding powders to be mixed into thunder dust. "This is not the fate I sought for myself."

"I know, Janos." Mica grimaced. "I have grown to enjoy peace." He rested his hand on his sword. "But I will not allow the Horde to enslave my family."

"Your children will be safe enough."

"I hope so."

"We have the fleet."

"And your thunder-hammers."

"Aye." Janos grunted sourly. "Would that we had not created such devices."

"They will prove our salvation."

"Or our damnation."

* * *

"Loose!"

Mica watched the arrows streak across the clearing. "Every shot near perfect on the target."

Janos blinked. "They are small targets."

"Aye, the size of a man's neck. What use in shooting at a torso when their armour will block the shot?" Mica watched the archers loose a second volley. "Better to aim where the armour is weak."

"I suppose." Janos paused. "Do you think we can hold?" he asked bluntly.

"Can Solace hold where Salidaralesom did not?"

"Yes."

"I'm not sure," Mica admitted. "But at least this time I have confidence that it will make the attempt."

* * *

The great fleet of the Elves was making ready to sail.

"But why can't I go?" Keff demanded.

"Because we need one of us to stay here." Janos watched a line of Elves carrying supplies onto one of the xebecs. The harbour was crowded with boats. "You and I know the secrets of thunder dust."

"Everyone knows those secrets now."

"But only we are the masters of those secrets. If I am lost," he swallowed nervously, "then you will be left to carry on our research."

"If you are lost, the defence of Solace will be up to Keff." Sapphire smiled, showing no sign of worry. "He will do his duty. We all will."

"I hope he doesn't get seasick again." Mica grinned. "Gods, I hope I don't."

Chapter Twenty-Two

"I hate ships."

"I know, Janos."

"I mean I really and truly *hate* ships." Janos was clutching at the rail as the deck heaved under his feet. "Why did I let you talk me into coming? I should have sent Keff. That fool *wanted* to come along on this voyage."

"You chose to come. Better to send the master." Mica stood loosely, moving with the motion of the waves. He wore Elf-style armour, the links of mail forged to fit his build, and carried his favoured sword.

The captain of the *Sea Wytch* smiled as he stepped past. "Drink more of the tea," Cerion pressed. "It will settle your stomach." The wind tugged at his blue cloak and his long hair with equal strength.

"I don't want the tea. It tastes even worse going down than it does coming back up." Janos shuddered. "I should know by now."

"And he carries Elf-Blood in his veins." Cerion laughed loudly. "Must have been Tunnel-Elf."

* * *

"Another day of endless water."

"What did you expect, Janos? To set sail and immediately encounter the Horde?" Mica laughed. He held a far-seer tube in his hand but did not use it.

"If we found that Horde that quickly, it would mean that the city would already be lost!" Cerion shook his head. "It is far from uncommon for opposing navies to sail for months seeking each other and not meeting."

"*Months?*" Janos wailed. "I cannot live for months on this Gods-damned ship!"

"We will not sail for months. There is no need. The Horde seeks the port of Solace...they will come to us."

"You sound confident."

"You forget that we are Sea Elves...the waves are as much home to us as the forests." Cerion glanced at the sky. "The currents talk to me. The wind whispers of black sails."

Janos lifted the far-seer tube to his eye and idly scanned the horizon. "Ye Gods!" he swore and almost dropped the tube from his fingers. "I see ships!"

"Ships?" Certion snatched the tube from Mica's hand. "Let me see."

The ships were dark against the horizon.

Janos lifted a far-seer tube to his eye. "I see their flags," he said grimly as he studied the blocky wooden hulls. "Keli'cairn." The ships were painted black and gray.

"Those are old Imperial galleons," Mica commented. "Probably captured when the city fell."

"And turned against us." Cerion chuckled. "And here I was dreading some serious danger. We can out sail those hulls with ease."

"Can we?"

"Aye. Our xebecs have swallows compared to those lumbering turkeys."

"They have numbers." Mica lowered his far-seer tube. "We must close with them to fight...they will have many more archers than we."

"We can handle them. We have the thundertubes."

"The Red Lightning Bolt is closing."

"Then we must prepare ourselves to fight." Cerion turned. "To arms!" he shouted. "To arms!"

Mica gestured to the crew. "Stand ready."

"So many ships," Janos breathed. He lowered the tube. "There are so bloody many!" He glanced over his shoulder as the Elf crew began hurrying about with purposeful movements.

"Look at one good thing," Mica said as a bell tolled out to warn the other Elf ships.

"What?"

"You're not complaining about your stomach anymore."

Janos rolled his eyes. "You find the oddest things amusing."

* * *

"They draw closer."

"Do they have the numbers to threaten Solace?"

"Aye," Cerion said, "though not as great as what is reported traveling by land...these are distraction." He spat over the side. "They are meant to keep our garrison in the city and not waylay the main Horde as it marches overland."

"A nasty scheme of theirs."

"Aye." The captain gestured. "Ready catapults!" The wind blew through his silvery hair. The entire fleet was sailing towards the black ships.

Janos gripped the rail. "Is this going to work?" he asked aloud as the sails were tied tightly and the xebecs accelerated towards the enemy navy.

"It *was* your idea," Mica reminded him.

"But I'm no admiral!"

"Nor am I."

"I'm having second thoughts."

"Release!" Cerion bellowed.

The catapults released their loads.

Pottery jugs hurtled through the air. Many of them missed the enemy galleons, sinking into the water with small splashes; a few hit and the pottery exploded with flame and sulphurous smoke.

"Reload!" Mica bellowed to the crew.

"The accuracy could be improved upon."

Cerion scanned the galleons with the far-seer tube. "Catapults are not known for their accuracy, Janos. Some things are beyond the scope of mortal men. And Elves," he added hastily.

"At least there's some fire." Mica smiled. "They cannot fight us and fires both."

The catapults flung a second volley at the Horde.

One of the galleons shuddered as numerous pottery jugs exploded against its hull. The ship began to sink.

"Sail into their midst." The captain gestured. "They are wavering."

"How can you tell?" Janos demanded as he tried to make sense of the shifting boats after what must have been hours of battle. "'Tis all confusion to me." He was hard-pressed to tell which ship was friend and which was foe. *And the screaming! Men do not die quietly.* "Do we have to close? Can't we continue to use the catapults?"

The captain took no notice. "Fire arrows ready." The archers took their places at the rail as Mica waved his sword at them. "Release!"

A flight of arrows pelted the closest galleon. Fires took hold in the sails and on the deck.

"We have their range!"

"And they have ours!" Mica warned as the Horde returned fire at last.

Janos cursed and ducked as fire arrows hissed into the sea around them. "They have a lot of arrows!" he warned.

"Did you expect otherwise?" Mica asked him. "You know how they favour their bows."

"That was on land." Janos gestured to the tattered remnants of the Horde. "We've dealt them a fearsome blow," he said. "The thunder dust has shattered much of their fleet. Why don't they withdraw?"

"Because they know that we can overtake them. They must stand and fight...or die."

Janos shook his head. "Warfare is a nasty business."

"Aye, that it is."

"Take us about!" Mica shouted. "Hit them again."

A fire arrow struck the mast.

"Douse those fire!" the captain bellowed. "Move, you dogs!"

"This is no place for a scholar!" Janos snatched up a bucket and hurled water onto a small fire. "No place at all."

The cries of survivors were growing fewer.

"They're drowning."

Janos hung on the rail, staring at the scene with horrified eyes. So many galleons were sinking under the waves, others were burning wrecks. The ocean was littered with broken pieces of wood and equally broken bodies. Some still moved, others clung to flotsam, most were floating lifelessly. "Captain, can we save any?"

"Do we want too?" he asked. "They are only barbarians."

"We are not monsters."

"As you wish." Cerion shouted orders to his crew and the ship turned towards a knot of survivors clinging to planks and barrels.

Janos gasped.

One of the survivors was a bedraggled-looking Elf.

Chapter Twenty-Three

The Elf looked at his captors with hatred. "You think that I fear death?" he demanded as he squeezed seawater out of his stained tunic. "Death will be a release from the misery of life."

Janos frowned. "He is a dark soul." Then he sneezed as the wind carried the stench of burned flesh and sulfur to his nose.

Cerion spat over the rail. "You have betrayed your people and our ways for petty power."

"I brought down the Empire," he boasted. "Now for the others."

"You shattered the Humans' empire...why threaten ours?"

The Elf turned and sneered. "What has the Empire done for *us*?" he demanded. "They have stolen our ancestral lands. Burned our homes. Slaughtered our herds. Pillaged our homeland. Raped our women." His eyes blazed with the fury of his hatred. "So let them suffer now! Let them burn!" He laughed bitterly. "Let them all burn!"

Janos eyed the torches nervously. They were crackled fiercely. *Words have power and his words are liable to spark an inferno.*

* * *

"The fleet was repulsed."

"A victory then."

"Aye, Elder. Many of the galleons have sunk to the bottommost depths. Only a handful fled back to port. We are safe from the Keli'cairn."

"Only from the sea-based Keli'cairn. I fear that the rest may yet come by land." Sunmantle gestured westward. "Our scouts bear word that they have found paths through the peaks at last."

"Another Elf traitor?"

"Or just superior numbers of scouts." The Council was still disturbed by the presence of an Elf traitor among the Horde's fleet.

"In either case, they *are* coming."

"We can't hold them back."

"No. We lack the numbers to halt the Horde...as well to erect a wall to hold back the sea."

"The sea will wear away any wall in time...as will the Horde. But we can't just give up." Janos shook his head. "I won't give up."

Sapphire looked at him. "We will stand at the walls of Solace. The city will stand."

"It has too."

* * *

"They're burning the farms." Smoke was rising from the west. Too much smoke.

"There be no one left out there." Ironhelm spat over the battlement.

"Burning for the sake of pleasure." Mica swore under his breath as he counted the plumes. "They treated our lands so as they passed."

"The last of the outriders have returned. The numbers of Keli'cairn are estimated at several thousand. We cannot hope to stand against such might."

"It is not the full might of the Horde. Only a fraction of the numbers that marched against Salidaralesom march against us now."

"A fraction is still thousands. We cannot match those numbers."

"Nor can we fall back to some other stronghold. Solace *is* our stronghold."

"If this city falls, then the rest of the eastern kingdoms will be vulnerable."

"Hillmen won't yield," Ironhelm boasted. "If yon Horde enter our mines, they be entombing themselves."

"And slaughtering you when come back to the surface for food and supplies."

Ironhelm grunted. "Aye, there is that."

* * *

"I don't see why we have to stay cooped up in the city."

"Because bad men are roaming in the forest." Janos tried to mask his fear in front of the children. "We're quite safe here. They cannot scale the walls or batter in our gates." At least he hoped not. *The Horde breached the defences of Salidaralesom easily enough from what stories I've heard. I can only trust that Solace is better defended.*

"But why do those men want to hurt us?"

"It is their nature, Marigold. Some men are never satisfied with what they have...they want what others have."

"Can't we share?"

"This goes beyond merely sharing, I fear." Janos looked up as Sapphire and Mica stepped into the room. "This is a time of grave crisis."

"There is a tenseness in the air."

"No doubt, Sapphire. Can you be surprised by that?"

"The Horde approach, but the Shining Walls have never fallen."

"They've never faced such a challenge before."

"I have confidence in our warriors and in your talents, Janos."

Janos sighed. "I do not know if the thunderdust can save us."

"It will have too."

Chapter Twenty-Four

"The Horde are coming!"

"Stand by!" Janos lifted a far-seer to his eye. "So bloody many of them." Mounted men by the hundreds...and many thousands more on foot.

"The Horde is more fearsome than I had dreamed." Keff tried to sound calm, but he was sweating. "So many warriors."

"You chose to return here before the siege."

"I couldn't allow my friends to die without me." Keff lowered the far-seer tube. "Although I now think that perhaps I was too hasty."

"Thunder throwers are ready." Ironhelm sounded calm as he stood on the battlements. Too calm.

Janos looked at him.

Ironhelm grunted. "I've led sorties against them. I've helped delay their advance...but they just keep coming."

"Ye Gods." Janos fingered his medallion nervously.

Horns blew out, and men shouted in their alien tongue.

"Light-Bearers protect us," Janos prayed.

"The City will hold!" Mica shouted and held his sword aloft. "The City will hold!"

"The City will hold!" the Elves shouted.

Mica's armour was gleaming and he waved his sword.

"You're enjoying this!"

"I am a soldier," Mica agreed, "but warfare is not a thing to be enjoyed...it is to be merely survived."

The Horde drew closer.

"Fire!"

The tubes belched forth smoke and flame.

Dirt fountained into the air, along with parts of bodies and horses.

Janos lowered the far-seer from his eye with a trembling hand as thunder echoed from the walls. "Ye Gods," he swore in an unsteady voice. "I did not think it would do that." He was winter-pale.

Mica took the tube from his friend's trembling fingers and used it to stare across the crater-pocked fields. "'Tis effective."

"Aye, 'tis." Ironhelm watched his crews hurrying to reload. "Careful ye louts!" he bellowed. "Yer gonna blow us all into the Blessed Realm."

"They're not even into arrow range yet."

"The tubes are ready for a second volley."

Janos shook his head and mumbled another prayer.

"Fire at will," Mica told the others.

"Still they come!" Janos was amazed. And absolutely horrified. A dozen volleys from the thunder tubes had torn the ground with flame and slaughtered countless men, and still the Horde marched on the city.

Arrows hissed over the walls.

Elf archers took aim and fired back. Every arrow claimed a horseman, but the second volley was just as heavy as the first had been. Several Elves fell.

"We cannot hold them."

"We must." Keff winced as the thunder-hammers roared forth flames once again. "We have no choice."

"Ye Gods."

Mica stood on one parapet in his armour. "Back!" he shouted in the Keli'cairn tongue. "Back into the wastelands!"

Arrows skipped from the stone blocks around him.

Mica leaped down from his perch. "Damn them!"

"A day of siege," Sunmantle said from his grove. "And the Shining Walls are still held."

"Aye. We have repulsed no less than four charges. The ground beyond the walls is bloody ruin."

"Such is the nature of war." Sunmantle sounded pained by the thoughts. "We will have much to rebuild in the days to come."

"Aye."

Thunder-hammers roared in the distance.

"Your weapons work?"

Keff nodded. "As deadly as promised...and as feared."

"Yet the Horde still strikes."

"Aye. They are far too dangerous to be repulsed easily. I am not certain we can hold for long."

"The Shining Walls have never fallen. They will not fall now."

* * *

"Another charge."

"Aye."

Janos shook his head. He was tired and worn from lack of sleep. "Is this the nature of war?" he asked, gesturing to the broken bodies strewn before the walls. "Is this the nature of death?"

"Aye...and it is the nature of this science."

"Ye Gods."

Sapphire turned to him. "This is what we sought to escape from. It followed us here."

"Such are the times we live in." Mica watched another volley tear apart the ground. "We do what we must."

Sapphire turned to survey the battlefield. "At what cost?" she asked. "At what cost?"

"Loose another volley!" Mica shouted. The Horde was milling at the edge of bowshot.

"What is happening?" Janos lowered the far-seer tube. "Are they going to charge?"

"I do not know." Mica frowned. "That worries me."

The thunder-throwers roared and arrows sought their prey.

At last the pounding was too fierce for even the vaunted Horde to stand. First lone men, then pairs, and then entire groups broke ranks and fled back towards the trees.

"Retreating," Mica breathed. "Thanks be to all the gods. Never did I dream to see the day when the Horde would turn tail and flee."

"Thanks be to the Light Bearers indeed." Janos felt ill.

"Thanks to you," Ironhelm told him. "For this be your doing."

Janos flinched.

* * *

The gates of the city opened and the battle stunned inhabitants emerged. They stood blinking at the sight that greeted their wondering eyes.

"'Tis a victory." Mica gestured with his sword.

Janos could only shake at his head as he gazed upon the broken bodies of the fallen. A faint haze of sulphurous smoke still came to his nostrils on the same wind that brought the cries of those merely wounded and the screams of injured horses. *What have I unleashed upon the world?* he wondered.

"A victory?" Sunmantle sounded as if he was in pain. "You would name this slaughter a victory?" His eyes were half closed and tears were running down his pale cheeks.

"What have we become?" Sapphire asked aloud. "By the Blessed Light Bearers...what have we become?"

"What we needed to be," Mica replied. "What the world made us."

Discover other titles by Matt Kirkby at Smashwords.com:
Connect with Me Online:
Smashwords: http://www.smashwords.com/profile/view/MattKirkby
Facebook: http://facebook.com/MattKirkby[1]
Facebook Fan-Page: Matt Kirkby's Facebook fan page[2]

---

1. http://www.facebook.com/people/Matt-Kirkby/700512171

2. http://www.facebook.com/pages/Matt-Kirkby/176584565711824

Also by Matt Kirkby

A Novel of Lovecraftian Horror
The Death of Hope

Stories Of Feudal Japan
With Honour Veiled

Standalone
A Wyrm In the Heart
Cthonian Dragons
Forlorn Gambit
Reap What Has Been Sown
The Horror From The Sea
Vector Of Infection

About the Author

Born and raised in small-town Ontario, Matt Kirkby is a romantic dreamer who specializes in writing tales of high fantasy and pulp-style science fiction and space operas. He draws his inspiration from all diverse sources and ideas: Science Fiction, Fantasy, Gothic Horror, Pastoral Nature. He started his writing career submitting fan fiction for numerous Star Wars and TransFormers fanzines, but has since moved on to writing professionally. He published his first novel, A Wyrm In The Heart in 2004. He lives a double life, writing classy sci-fi and fantasy for fun under his own name, and penning gay erotica under the pen name of Frank Sol. When not writing, Matt spends his time helping his partner with his hand-crafted rocking chair business -- www.OffYourRocker.ca -- and trying to maintain some control over his cat. He still thinks that no gift is better than a new book.